> ## "I remember when you thought I was pretty great."

"We all have our delusions," Harper began. "And—"

"And I thought you were pretty great," Dillon went on. Then his eyes perused her face, moving from feature to feature as though she were brand-new to him.

Harper's breath began to come in gasps. "But not great enough to spend a lifetime with."

He sighed quietly. "You're always so into defining everything, telling me what it must or mustn't be."

"I would think that'd make sense to a doctor. How can you treat something if you haven't diagnosed it, determined what it is?"

He leaned a little closer. "Love's not an illness, Harper. It's supposed to be an adventure."

"You can't run through love blindly," she insisted, distracted by the nearness of his mouth. "It's all very...complicated."

He considered that, and her. Then he caught the back of her head in his hand and drew her toward him. "Let me simplify it for you."

Dear Reader,

Okay. I'm hooked on babies. As the Jensen-Baker families swell with more and more grandchildren for Ron and me, I'm able to study and adore them while being removed from the responsibility of parenthood.

Julia is our newest addition to the family, a sturdy, bright little bundle who just had her first birthday. I've always thought she was so beautiful she should have been twins—and a writer's personal life always ends up in her books.

So I began to imagine what would have happened if Julia had been twins born to a woman who was unable at that point in time to provide for them. What would become of them?

Enter the pulse of every romance novel—the hero.

The twins' mother would send them to their father, but who was he? My imagination created three possibilities, and when I couldn't decide among them, the McKeon brothers were born.

Now with three heroines to provide the spark each brother is missing in his life, I leave you to decide why the mother left her babies, and WHO'S THE DADDY? Darrick, the hospital administrator; Dillon, the orthopedist; or Duncan, the actor?

Muriel Jensen

Muriel Jensen
Daddy By Design

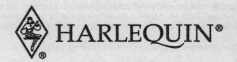

HARLEQUIN®

TORONTO • NEW YORK • LONDON
AMSTERDAM • PARIS • SYDNEY • HAMBURG
STOCKHOLM • ATHENS • TOKYO • MILAN • MADRID
PRAGUE • WARSAW • BUDAPEST • AUCKLAND

To Betty Cier,
stand-in mom and friend forever.

ISBN 0-373-16742-3

DADDY BY DESIGN

Printed in U.S.A.

Prologue

September

Dillon McKeon told himself that he should never have taken Harper into his arms. But he'd wanted to prove to himself that he was over her. That after fifteen months without her he'd evolved into someone she could no longer affect with her wide hazel eyes, small, perfect body, her bewitching wit and spirit. That he could dance with her at his parents' anniversary party for old times' sake, then walk away when the music stopped.

Now he was a victim of his own prideful need to prove something. He could feel every warm curve of her against him, recall as though they'd left their bed only moments ago what it had been like to make love with her.

And, God help him, he wanted to do that again right now even more than he wanted to draw his next breath.

What was worse—she'd leaned into him before the first bar of music floated away across the room. She'd pretended indifference at first, smiling when he greeted her, casually accepting his offer to dance, but holding herself purposefully away from him as he took her into his arms.

Then the band had started a slow, bluesy version of "It Had to be You"—their song—and she'd slipped an arm around his neck, tipped her head into his shoulder and closed the distance between them.

"WHAT AM I DOING? What am I *doing?!*"

Harper Harriman felt her resolve slip away in the harbor of Dillon's arms. She'd been so certain that dancing with him would be easy because she'd put him out of her life. She'd accepted rationally that no matter how good they were together in some ways, there were others in which he just couldn't fit into her life—now, particularly. He had always been gone, had always *loved* to be gone, had always found an excuse to be gone again.

She tried to list in her mind all the reasons they'd parted, even as the tender confidence of his embrace reminded her of one of the reasons she'd regretted their break-up: He always seemed to know what he was doing. In a life that had been largely insecure, she had found that so admirable.

And when they weren't fighting, he was the sweetest man she'd ever known.

"Harper," she heard him whisper as he wrapped both arms around her swaying to the music and the telling lyrics: "...*finally found...make me be true... make me be blue.*"

She joined her fingers behind his neck as his arms drew her closer. Then she looked up into his eyes. And there it was—love. It burned clearly in his gaze, the perfect reflection of everything she felt. It wasn't dead at all—in him or in her.

He stopped moving to the music and whispered urgently, "Come home with me."

She wanted to. Desperately. "Dillon, I have to—" she began.

He interrupted her with a hand to her cheek, a thumb running lightly over her bottom lip. "You have to be with me. I have to be with you. That's all we have to know right now."

She parted her lips to continue, but he took advantage of the small movement to kiss her again. The dancers around them stopped to look, but he didn't seem to notice. "Will you come?" he asked breathlessly, lifting his head.

"Yes." As she looked into his dark, loving eyes, she could remember only one word in her entire vocabulary. "Yes. Yes."

They were at his place on the edge of Edenfield in ten minutes, and they undressed each other on their way to the bedroom.

Then they were body to body in the old maple double bed, cool sheets enfolding them as they relearned the topography of each other's bodies—silken curves and planes, graceful lines, tight muscle, inviting hollows.

They came together like a lock and its key, the world opening under their movements to reveal new treasures and new truths.

It was morning before they fell asleep in each other's arms, exhausted.

Harper woke to the ringing of the telephone. She lay stiffly as Dillon answered. She'd always sworn she could tell the difference in the ring when a call came from the Northwest Medical Team of which Dillon was a part.

The pain began in the pit of her stomach as she watched him listen to the caller, then spread to her heart. She knew the drill. In a moment he would say, "I'll be right there," and everything between them would be erased from his mind as he prepared to join the other members of his team to take off on a lifesaving mission.

She climbed out of bed and pulled on her blue silk dress.

Still on the phone, Dillon caught her arm as she walked by him on a search for her shoes. She pulled away from him as she found one in his bedside chair, and the other under it. She sat down to slip them on.

"I'll be right there," he said into the receiver, then turned off the cordless phone and tossed it on the bed.

"A mud slide in the Philippines," he said.

She nodded and tried to push past him, but he caught her arms. "Come on, Harp," he cajoled. "I know how you are about the team, but you can't just walk away after last night."

"Why not?" she asked, meeting his eyes. "*You* can."

His jaw tightened and his expression hardened. "It's not the same thing."

"I know." She shook her head sadly. "I'm selfish and you're heroic. We've been here before, Dillon."

He dropped his hands and turned away in complete exasperation. "God! How can you look like you do and still be six years old inside? I'm through fighting about this! How can we have spent so much time together and have affected each other so little?"

She felt an hysterical need to laugh, but the tears came first.

She grabbed up her purse and left him—again.

Chapter One

Memorial Day weekend, the following year

It was good to be home. Dillon smiled and stretched wearily as he drove past the Welcome to Dancer's Beach sign. Actually, the little beach town wasn't home yet, but it would be soon.

Last fall, Dillon and his brothers had bought an old house here to use as a summer retreat. Duncan, the oldest, was a successful actor, with an elaborate place in Malibu, who sought rest and anonymity between films. At the moment he was somewhere in Africa.

Darrick, the middle McKeon brother, was administrator of a hospital in Edenfield, Oregon, just south of Portland, and spent all his free time with a golf club in one hand and a fishing pole in the other.

Dillon was an orthopedist who ran a clinic in Edenfield in partnership with several friends, and donated a considerable amount of time to the Northwest Medical Team, a crisis response group. He'd just flown in to the Portland Airport last night after six weeks in Nicaragua, where the team had helped victims of an earthquake outside Matagalpa.

Dillon took a deep breath of salty air and thought

how fresh and clean it smelled after the oppressive odors of Nicaragua's dampness, rotting vegetation and crowded hospitals.

He listened to the roll of the surf, the call of a seagull, then smiled again. Peace. He was so ready for four weeks of nothing to do but buy furniture for the summerhouse.

Before he and his brothers had split up last fall to go their separate ways, they'd stood on the porch steps and divided the duties of making the place comfortable.

Darrick, who had the first vacation, was to paint the interior and fix the small hole in the roof. He was the most logical and reliable of the three brothers. Dillon was sure Darrick had had it all done by the time their parents arrived for this Memorial Day weekend, which was also their father's birthday.

Dillon was to use the resources they'd pooled to buy furniture. He was looking forward to the task. He was also an orthopedist where furniture was concerned: he loved to rebuild and refinish old pieces. They didn't have to be valuable antiques, either, just old things with abused or broken parts.

Duncan had a gift for gardening, and was responsible for landscaping and buying lawn furniture. He was expected home at the end of June or early July.

Dillon glanced into the rearview mirror to check the picnic table he'd bought in McMinnville on his way to the coast. He was probably usurping part of Duncan's job, but he'd driven right by a discount store and had spotted the table placed out in front with several other sale items. A tent sign on it boasted a ridiculously low price. He'd stopped and bought it along with the two accompanying benches. The happy clerk had helped him tie them into the back of his old pickup.

Satisfied that they were still solidly tied, he followed the turn in the road and spotted the white house in the distance. It sat back about thirty yards and up on a little knoll. And it had been painted!

He knew the Realtor had agreed to contract someone for them, but it was still a pleasant surprise to see the bright white of fresh paint on the wide two-story with its full front porch that wrapped around on the north side. He could pick out the center gables on the first and second floors, and the openwork porch railing interrupted at ten-foot intervals by elegant columns.

As he drew closer, he noticed the green shutters and trim. He also noticed Darrick's white luxury sedan in the driveway, and his parents' car with a trailer attached. He couldn't help the low laugh that erupted from him, and the anticipation of the warmth and good cheer that always defined their family gatherings.

He knew his mother would look into his eyes to assess his emotional health. He would have to tell her everything he'd eaten in Nicaragua and then explain in detail how he felt physically and spiritually.

His father would check over his truck, possibly even wash it, and tell him for the tenth time that he should trade it in for something newer and safer.

Dori would hug him ferociously, then remind him that he hadn't written to her once during her year at Oxford and that, generally, he was a terrible communicator.

Darrick would give him that quick once-over glance that took in everything. But he wouldn't berate or criticize. He'd wait until Dillon brought up a problem, then he would offer the perfect solution. And Dillon would want to kill him.

Those thoughts ran through Dillon's mind as he

parked the truck behind the U-Haul and wondered why on earth he was eager to put himself in the middle of all that. But he didn't wonder seriously or for very long. In his family, meddling meant they all loved and cared about one another. They had no concept of individual freedom or the theory of "live and let live." They cajoled, harassed and bullied until you did what they thought was best for you.

Except in the case of Harper Harriman.

Harper. He could feel his blood pressure rise at the very thought of her. When he'd told his family that it was over between them and that he didn't want to answer any questions about it, they'd actually respected his wishes. He'd been shocked and, frankly, suspicious.

Then he remembered that during his engagement to Harper his family had grown almost as close to her as they were to him. And that Harper and his mother and his sister always kept in close touch. They probably didn't have to hear from *him* that Harper had packed all his clothes and shipped them to the Seattle offices of the Northwest Medical Team, claiming that there was no point in keeping them at home since he was never there. And that in retaliation, he'd nailed all her doors and windows closed before he moved out, leaving her a note that said he could think of no other way to assure her of the security she craved.

Harper had probably told his mother and Dori everything, and they in turn had passed it on to everyone else in the family. Well, that was good because he didn't want to talk about it—ever. Harper the Harridan was out of his life and good riddance.

Dillon strolled up the driveway and the front porch steps, then tried the front door. Locked. Of course. When his mother was around, doors were always locked to protect them from terrorists, thieves, and the odd random lunatic.

He pulled out his keys, found the shiny gold-colored one he'd never used before, and fitted it into the lock.

The sound of laughter and loud conversation came to him from the back of the house. He ignored it for a moment as he took in the freshly painted white living room with its carved fireplace and beautifully arched molding in the dining room doorway. The last time he'd seen it, it had been a dingy lavender.

An obviously used but comfortable-looking brocade loveseat sat in the middle of the room, and several odd chairs—*really* odd—were clustered around it as though ready to encourage conversation.

All *right,* he thought, feeling the same sense of rightness he'd experienced the first time he'd walked into this house. It *was* home. Already.

"Hi!" he called, striding toward the dining room. "I picked up a picnic table at Costmart. Can somebody help me?" He stopped abruptly as he caught sight of what appeared to be an old horse collar hanging over the fireplace as if it were the centerpiece of the room. Someone had had the appalling notion of putting a clock in the circle formed by the fat leather loop.

The creative part of him was horrified. But he smiled as the McKeon part of him guessed where it had come from. His parents. The antiquers from hell. The dearest, kindest people who fell in love with the ugliest and most atrocious remnants from another time. Suddenly he couldn't wait to see them.

He went through the dining room, admiring its fresh paint, as he called, "Darrick? Dad?"

Dillon stopped suddenly in the doorway because the first face he saw, he didn't recognize. It was female and quite beautiful, with blue eyes and surrounded by a thick mass of dark hair. Darrick had his arm around her and she was holding a baby.

She smiled tentatively at Dillon.

He was about to reach a hand out to her to introduce himself when he noticed that another woman stood several feet away from her. She was small but shapely in khaki shorts and a chambray shirt.

Short hair the color of a star was shaped in a ragged cut to frame startled hazel eyes, a small, straight nose, and full fuchsia-pink lips whose soft contours brought a thousand unwelcome memories flooding into his awareness.

Before he could defend himself against them, they became so real that he could feel her lips on his eyelids, on his mouth, at his throat, working down the middle of his chest and over his waist.

Harper.

"No," he heard himself say quietly, plaintively. It was a response to the memories and not to her, but he immediately saw the startled look in her eyes changing to one of hurt. She'd never been one to give an uncertain moment time to sort itself out.

"Hello, Dillon," she said airily, though he saw her take a quick swallow. "Try to be civilized, okay? We have an audience."

There was an instant of tense silence, then he opened his mouth to explain his surprise. But Darrick left the pretty brunette to come and take Dillon in a bear hug. "Don't mind us," he said dryly with a grin at Harper. "You two have been fighting so long the rest of us just wait around for the next instalment of the drama." He gave Dillon an affectionate clap on the back. "How are you? You put everybody back together?"

Before Dillon could answer the question, he was swarmed over by the rest of his family, and kissed, hugged, questioned, as he was passed from his mother, to Dori—who also held a baby—to his father.

Then his mother took over again, pulling him toward the pretty brunette back in Darrick's arm. She was a little disheveled but glowing, he noticed, as though she'd just been through something traumatic and had risen victorious.

"We have all kinds of...surprises for you!" his mother said, her cheerful manner just a little forced.

No kidding, he thought, carefully keeping his eyes from Harper. He'd been so looking forward to this weekend with his family and he refused to admit to himself that Harper's presence was going to ruin it for him.

But he reasoned, they would all be going home on Monday and he would finally have the place to himself. He'd get his peace after all. He could put up with Harper until then. Especially if he could lock her in a closet.

"Dillon, these are your neighbors," his mother said, "Cliff and Bertie Fisher. They live in the yellow house over the hill."

Dillon shook hands with a cheerful and smiling older couple, the woman short and plump, the man taller and graying.

"Our daughter was your Realtor," Bertie said. "She told us three handsome young men had bought the Buckley house. But I hadn't realized how handsome."

"Thanks, Bertie," Darrick teased. "You never said that to *me*."

Bertie gave him a friendly shove with her elbow. "Oh, now, you're gorgeous and you know it. But your brother looks dangerous.'' She smiled at Dillon with a look that told him Cliff probably had his hands full. "It's no secret that women like that. Even old women.''

"Don't fall for her line, son," Cliff said gravely. "I did and I've been nothing but her plaything ever since.''

Dillon laughed, liking both of them. "A noble fate," he said.

"And this," his mother went on with a Vanna White-esque wave of her arms, "is your new sister-in-law, Skye Fennerty McKeon, Darrick's wife. She's a pilot. Skye, this is Darrick's younger brother, Dillon.''

Dillon shelved the problem of Harper for a moment and stared in amazement. He'd only been away a few weeks...

His sister-in-law laughed as she gave Dillon a spontaneous hug. "Hi!" she said warmly. "It's wonderful to meet you at last. I understand you're a brilliant chef.''

"Ah...brilliant might be a little strong," he said, holding her at arm's length, appreciating Darrick's impeccable taste in women. Trust him to find a woman who was beautiful *and* sweet. "You're an airline pilot?''

"No. I run a little flight service in Mariposa, California.'' Her expression turned suddenly rueful. "I'm sure you remember when Darrick was trying to get home for your parents' anniversary party and crashed in the Siskiyous?''

Dillon remembered the family's panic when Darrick hadn't arrived on schedule. It had been a long night of trying to track his change of plans, finally relieved the following morning when Darrick called to report that he'd survived a forced landing in a light plane and was on his way.

"You were flying the plane that crashed?" he asked.

She corrected pleasantly, "I was flying the plane that landed your brother safely in the woods."

"In a tree," Darrick added.

She glared at him teasingly.

He pretended innocence. "Just getting the story straight."

She turned back to Dillon. "Anyway, I ran the flight service out of Mariposa until Darrick arrived with the...twins." Her smile waned a little and she sent Darrick an uncomfortable glance.

Dillon turned to his brother. His mother certainly had been right about surprises. He grinned. "Twins?" He pointed from Skye to Darrick as he stepped closer to peer at the baby. "You two have twins?"

Darrick gave him a steady look, opened his mouth as though to reply, then changed his mind. There was a protracted silence.

Dillon shifted his weight, trying to understand. "They're *not* your twins?"

"No."

"Whose are they?"

Everyone looked at everyone else, then all eyes seemed to settle on Darrick. Dillon didn't know why, but he found himself taking a defensive posture. He turned slowly toward Harper.

She met his eyes, her own lethal. Then she scooped the baby from Darrick and walked out of the room, headed for the stairs, murmuring something about changing a diaper. Dori followed her with the other baby. His father said he had to fire up the barbecue, and that seemed to require his mother and the Fishers to help.

Dillon now stood alone in the kitchen with Darrick and Skye. "All right," he said, a weird sense of trepidation playing along his spine. "What's going on?"

"I'll go upstairs and...um..." Skye backed toward the doorway to the stairs. "Make the bed."

"We have beds?" Dillon asked. "I thought I was supposed to buy furniture."

Darrick nodded. "You are. She means the sleeping bag."

"She's going upstairs to 'make' the sleeping bag?"

Darrick blew a kiss at Skye. "Go ahead. In his defense, he's usually not this stupid." To Dillon, he said, "She's trying to give us privacy so we can talk."

From the doorway, Skye sent Dillon a smile that seemed composed of sympathy and a little sadness. "Nice to meet you, Dillon," she said and disappeared upstairs.

Dillon frowned at Darrick, his skin prickling with the sudden certainty that however much he craved peace and quiet, he wasn't going to get it. His family was behaving strangely. While that wasn't unusual in itself, this particular strangeness had an air of potential trouble about it. "Darrick, what the hell is going on?" he demanded.

Darrick pointed him to the kitchen table and pulled a couple of mugs out of the cupboard. "Want some coffee?"

Dillon pulled out a chair and sat. "Sure."

Dillon watched Darrick pour with the easy grace he'd always envied. He'd always thought Darrick would have made a good surgeon because of his economy of movement and his steadiness, but his brother had been more interested in the workings of business than the workings of the body.

He brought his mind back to the question at hand as Darrick handed him a steaming mug of coffee and sat across from him. A sudden ugly thought struck him.

"Is somebody ill?"

Darrick reassured him with a quick shake of his head. "No. Everybody's fine."

"Then, what? It's something to do with the twins?" He leaned back in his chair as another alarming thought formed. "Are they Dori's?"

"No." Darrick folded his arms on the table and met Dillon's gaze. He wore the same expression, Dillon thought, that he'd worn all those years ago when he'd told him Donovan had died. "They could be yours."

It took Dillon a full minute to absorb the impact of the words. His. *His.* The small word vibrated around him like the sound of cymbals in a closet.

He struggled for coherent thought, for reason.

"They were born at Valley Memorial on May 10th," Darrick said in a slow, calm voice, "to a woman called Rachel Whitney, who abandoned them the following day. She—"

Dillon shot out of the morass of his thoughts like a rocket, his muddled mind suddenly free. "I don't even know a Rachel Whitney," he said. "I've never heard…"

When Darrick's expression didn't change, Dillon felt the fog close in on him again. "That was an alias," Darrick said.

"What?"

"It wasn't her real name."

Dillon leaned toward his brother impatiently. "I know what an *alias* is, but I don't understand why a woman would have babies using one. What's the point? I mean, if she was claiming I was the father, wouldn't she have used McKeon as the alias?''

"She used D. K. McKeon as the father's name on the birth certificate,'' Darrick explained.

Dillon took a quick sip of coffee. "But we're *all* D. K. McKeon. They could be yours. Or Duncan's.''

Darrick nodded. "I thought they were mine.'' He leaned back in his chair and folded his arms. "I was at a conference on hospital security the weekend the twins were born, and when I got back the staff was waiting for me, thinking, because of the name on the birth certificate, that some woman I'd impregnated and left to her fate was paying me back by leaving the babies to me.''

Dillon did a moment's calculations. "But Maddie had already dumped you. Who...?''

"Skye,'' Darrick replied. "The night we crashed in the mountains, we—'' he hesitated, then grinned "—kept warm.''

Dillon would have grinned in response, but he thought suddenly that he knew where this was going— and he didn't like it. He thought harder, desperate for an out.

"But that makes just a little over eight months.''

"The twins came early.''

"Without RDS? jaundice?''

Darrick shook his head. "No respiratory distress syndrome. No jaundice. You saw them. They're perfect.''

"Oh, God.'' Dillon ran a hand down his face as a very possible scenario formed in his mind—a scenario that could very well mean the twins *were* his.

Darrick studied him empathetically. "They could be

Duncan's," he said, "but he's been out of the country so much this past year."

"Oh, God," Dillon said again, the fervor of prayer behind the words.

Darrick sat forward, leaning his arms on the table again. "What? You think they *are* yours?"

Dillon closed his eyes, remembering Harper and the night of his parents' anniversary party. No. This couldn't be. Surely if a pregnancy had resulted from that night, she'd have told him. Surely if Harper was the mother of the twins, she wouldn't have abandoned them?

But she'd been in Seattle for the past year, and he hadn't seen her once. And while there'd been a time when he'd have sworn she didn't have a selfish, vindictive bone in her body, he'd since had proof to the contrary.

"I think they *could* be mine," he said, looking Darrick in the eye as he pushed away from the table. "Excuse me."

HARPER HURRIEDLY PACKED the few things she'd brought with her. Dori and Skye watched, each pacing and bouncing a sleepy baby.

"This is ridiculous!" Dori said, pulling on the T-shirt with Betty Boop on it that Harper tried to put into her bag. "I like that and I haven't gotten to borrow it yet."

Harper relinquished it and stuffed her makeup bag in on top. "It's yours."

"But how are you going to get home?" Skye asked. "You rode with Peg and Charlie."

"I'll take a cab to the airport," Harper answered, zipping the functional gym bag closed. "Wait till I get my hands on your mother. She told me she was sure Dillon wouldn't make it back this weekend.''

"The airport is sixty miles away!''

"I've got a company card. I'll write it off.''

Michelle, in Skye's arms, began to fuss.

"Harper, you can't leave," Skye said gently, standing squarely in her path as Harper shouldered her purse and picked up her bag. "Michelle's really gotten attached to you.''

Harper sighed, put the bag down, and leaned over the babies as Skye and Dori stood side by side. She'd grown attached to the twins, too, and would miss them. But now that Dillon was home, she couldn't stay. And he'd made it more than clear that he didn't want her to.

Her features softened as she touched first one tufty dark head, then the other. "Be good babies," she cooed softly. "Even if Dillon is your daddy, you're beautiful and precious enough to survive such misfortune. And I'll be thinking about you—''

"Harper!'' The sound of a man's voice came sharply from the doorway.

She straightened and turned to see Dillon standing there, looking like a thundercloud. She'd always thought him the most handsome of the McKeons, and her anger with him hadn't altered that view.

All the brothers had the same dramatic, dark coloring and the long, lean frames from which a woman's dreams were spun. Darrick was good-looking in a Wall Street three-piece-suit sort of way, and Duncan had the beautifully sculpted eyebrows and the square jaw of a matinee idol.

But Dillon had the bad-boy looks—hair always a

little too long, eyes a little too frank, mouth a little too full.

And the fact that he wasn't a bad boy at all, but a man completely devoted to his work, only contributed to his mystique.

She'd fallen for it twice. And that had been more than enough.

"I'd like to talk to you," he said, glancing cursorily past her at Skye and Dori. "Excuse us. I'm going to take her away for a minute."

"No, you're not." Harper picked up her bag. "I'm leaving." She turned to smile sadly at her friends. "Come and visit me."

Dillon stood squarely in the doorway as Harper walked toward it. "You're not going anywhere," he said, "until we've talked."

"Really." She raised an eyebrow and met his direct glare. "I seem to recall you told me you were through talking to me."

"That was about my work. This is another matter."

"Well, whatever it is," she said, trying to push past him, "I don't feel like talking about it."

He didn't budge. "Whatever it is?" He repeated her words with indignant disbelief, and for a moment she was confused.

And that moment was all it took for him to take the bag from her, toss it back into the room, and haul her with him down the stairs.

She pulled against him, grabbing at his fingers.

He turned, put a shoulder to her waist and tipped her over it.

She yelped in surprise, then delivered a fierce kidney punch he didn't even seem to notice.

She was aware of his parents and the neighbors going by upside down as Dillon strode to the front door.

"Charlie!" she implored, pushing against Dillon's back to raise her head and upper body. "Do something!"

Charlie shook his head. "Never could do anything with that boy."

Then Harper's eyes were skimming over the pebbles in the walk, the blacktop of the road, beach grass that eventually thinned out and disappeared leaving only sand. And that was where Dillon finally stopped.

He set her on her feet several yards from the ocean and held her arms a moment to steady her.

She erupted upright, arms swinging like a windmill. "You amoeba-brained, prehistoric, bug-eating—!"

"Yeah, yeah, yeah," he said, catching her wrists and holding them still until she was forced to look at him. "I want to know about the twins."

Her first instinct was to kick him in the shins and run. But there was another, more powerful instinct at work. She wasn't sure how to define it, but it was some touch-memory that took the grip of his angry hands and turned the feeling into the tender touch he used to use to stop her when she walked past his chair and to pull her into his lap.

Their nights together came back to her with the vivid purity of favorite recollections—firelit evenings, popcorn and wine, the feeling of being held in the hollow of his shoulder as they watched an old movie or listened to music. Even their one-night reunion had left her with haunting memories.

For a moment they were so sweet that she forgot she and Dillon had become enemies.

"What about the twins?" she asked breathlessly.

"Are they ours?" he demanded sharply.

The sweet memory dissolved instantly and she had to fight the flood of color to her face, fight any betrayal of guilt.

"No, they're not *ours,*" she replied as sharply, yanking free of him. Yes, he'd expect anger from her. "What woman in her right mind would have a baby with *you?*"

She turned to trudge through the sand to the road, but he caught her wrist again and pulled her back. "The timing's right," he said, his tone a little less angry, a little more defensive. "There was that night of my parents' party."

She stood impassive under his hold, telling herself that she had it all under control. All she had to do was remain calm. "If you recall," she said, "we talked about the risk and I told you I had protection."

Unfortunately there'd been no protection against the emotional risk.

"But you wanted me to quit the medical team and settle down." He spoke the words mildly, so she missed the implication until he finished the thought. "You could have been setting me up for fatherhood so you could finally have the nine-to-five husband you've always wanted."

Harper hit him in the middle of his chest with her open hand and shoved him as hard as she could. And this was no act. In her temper, however, she forgot that he still held her other hand in his. When he jerked backward, she went, too, and slammed up against him.

But this time there was no warm memory of being held by him. All she knew was fury, resentment, regret.

"What a *despicable* thing to say!" she shrieked at him. "And stupid as well! If that had been my plan, wouldn't I have told you the moment I was pregnant? Wouldn't I have been feathering my nest all this time? Would I have abandoned my babies in the hospital instead of telling you that you were about to be a father?''

It was apparent by the sudden shift in his expression that he hadn't considered that.

Harper took advantage of the quiet to press her point home. The purse she'd slung over her shoulder when she'd intended to leave the cottage was still in place. She delved into it for the photos of her new studio that she'd brought to show Peg and Charlie.

She sorted through them until she found the right photo—the one of herself and Wade taken two months previously for the new promotional brochure.

She pointed to her slender image in a form-fitting, mid-calf-length woolen dress. ''See that?'' she demanded.

''Yes,'' Dillon replied stiffly.

She turned the photo over to point to the date applied by the photo shop that had developed her film. ''April 11. I'd have been big as a house then if the twins were mine.''

She replaced the pictures in her purse again and adjusted the bag on her shoulder. ''You may very well have fathered Michelle and Gabrielle,'' she said, her voice irregular with anger, ''but you didn't do it with me. Goodbye.''

And she headed for the house to call a cab.

Chapter Two

"How can a taxi service have all its cars out of commission?" Harper demanded of Peg, who was taking the suitcase Harper had retrieved and placing it in a corner of the kitchen. "That's impossible! I don't believe you called."

As Harper stood in the middle of the room, Peg put a bib apron on her. It was very large and had to be looped twice around her waist. "Darling, this is a small town, remember? Seattle probably has hundreds of cabs, but Dancer's Beach has two. They tell me one's in the garage waiting for a part, and the other is taking a fare to Portland." Having tied the apron strings around Harper's waist, Peg smiled. "You're welcome to call them yourself if you don't believe me, and I promise not to be offended by the suggestion that I'd lie to you."

Harper groaned, knowing Peg had effectively backed her into a corner. Still, she had to get out of here.

"The cab taking the fare to Portland is expected back late tonight, so you can—"

"Late tonight?" Harper repeated. "It's only sixty-some miles to Portland."

"The fare has hired the cab for the day, Harper."

Peg patted her cheek. "Anyway, I don't see why you can't just enjoy barbecue with us, relax and chat for a while, and call the cab later tonight. You promised to make your layered salad, remember? I even brought my big glass bowl to show it off in."

Harper eyed her suspiciously. "Peg," she said, "I'm not sweet Skye who listens to everything you say and takes it as gospel. I've been around you McKeons for a while and I know what a conniver you are."

Peg's smile widened as she went to the refrigerator. "Then you should be taking notes. There comes a time in every woman's life when connivance is her most useful tool."

Harper caught the head of lettuce Peg tossed at her. "Women of my generation don't work that way anymore. No tricks and no games. We're honest... mostly."

Peg looked at her over the refrigerator door, her expression horrified. "Well, that just takes all the fun out of life. Men are predatory, remember. To catch one you have to beat him at his own game. And the hunt is all about attack and evasion. Tricks. Maneuvers. Strategies."

Resigned to her fate, at least for the afternoon, Harper placed the lettuce on the counter and rummaged through cupboards for a colander.

"But I'm not hunting, Peg. I'm flattered that you'd like me in the family, but I want nothing to do with your son."

When Peg didn't answer, Harper turned away from the cupboard, a battered metal colander in hand, to see what the older woman was doing. She was just in time to see a bag of frozen peas sail through the air toward her.

She caught it deftly in the colander.

Peg grinned. "You're too good at this *not* to play the game," she said.

Harper looked away before Peg could see in her eyes how right she was.

DILLON LEANED OVER the twins—asleep side by side in the portable crib, their tiny fingers entwined—and marveled at the miracle of life.

His friends always thought it interesting that new life amazed him when, as a doctor, he saw it again and again. But since he spent so much time in developing countries, he understood how vulnerable life itself was to the threats of disease and prenatal problems the American medical community had virtually eliminated.

He'd also seen the mistakes nature could make, the cruel tricks it could play, the devastation it could wreak in a matter of seconds. Babies paid a terrible price at those times.

So these two perfect little specimens were a blessing and a reason for thanks. The possibility that they were his made him even more awed and grateful.

But what was he going to do with month-old twins?

"Can you tell them apart yet?" Darrick followed his quietly spoken question onto the sunporch.

Dillon straightened. "Only because of the red fingernail. Dori told me the nurses had done that with Skin Scribe when you first brought them home. We still do it. That's Michelle," he added, pointing.

"Right. She's also a little fussier, a little more high-strung. Gabrielle's pretty laid-back."

Dillon looked up at his brother with fresh interest. It was amazing, he thought, that despite their growing up together just three years apart—sharing a room and clothes and toys and eventually their meager under-standing of girls—there were apparently things about Darrick he didn't know. Things that surprised him.

"You sound," he said, "as though you enjoyed your brief fatherhood."

Darrick smiled, and Dillon noted that his brother's expression when he looked down at the twins was ac-cepting but sad. "I thought they were mine. It was terrifying at first, but I got to love it—and them." Then Darrick looked up. "Did your talk with Harper clear up the mystery? Are they yours?"

Dillon sighed and went to the window through which he could see the backyard and the hills beyond. His father and Cliff were laughing together as they blew lightly on the thin spiral of smoke that signaled the beginning of a fire in the barbecue.

"They might be mine," he said, "but they're not Harper's. She showed me a photo of herself taken in April and she was definitely not pregnant."

Darrick came to lean a shoulder against the other side of the window frame. "You were in Zaire last September."

Dillon nodded.

"Not exactly a romantic spot."

Dillon nodded again. "It isn't romance that inspires lovemaking in a place like that. You do it because it's life-affirming, and because no matter how many times you've seen brutality and starvation up close, it never becomes understandable. It makes you feel alien and sort of…dead."

The room was thick with silence for a moment, then Darrick said, a note of humor in his voice, "Well, this time, apparently, it was life-affirming in the deepest sense."

Dillon had to smile. "Yes." Had Darrick asked him who the woman was, he might not have responded. But Darrick didn't, so Dillon volunteered the information. "Allison Cartier was there, too," he said.

Darrick repeated the name, then, after a moment's pause, raised an eyebrow. "The Cable Daily News Allison Cartier?"

"Right."

"Beautiful woman. Always looks so compelling in her flak jacket and that red hair. Temper to match?"

Dillon straightened away from the window, remembering the night he and Allison had spent together in London on their way home after three grueling weeks in the refugee camp. The machete wounds had been unspeakable, the separated families heart-wrenching, the conditions deplorable.

He remembered that they'd needed each other so much that night, but now he felt no sense of loss at her absence.

"No. No temper," he replied. "Just a sharp intelligence, a very welcome sense of humor, and a lust for the next story and where it would take her." He shook his head, his gaze unfocused. "I remember so appreciating that about her, because Harper and I had broken up months before because she hated that *I* moved around so much."

"I suppose after growing up among five aunts who were always on the run, she's looking forward to a simple, stay-at-home kind of life."

That was precisely what had broken them up. Then four days after Dillon's encounter with Allison, he had arrived at his parents' anniversary party to find Harper there and had fallen for those eyes and that beautiful little body all over again. Only to discover the next morning that passion might have reignited but that nothing had been resolved between them.

"Yeah. Well. That's not me."

"Wait a minute," Darrick said, frowning. "Wouldn't we have noticed on the air that Allison was pregnant?"

Dillon shook his head, thinking how cleverly fate plotted their lives. "Haven't you noticed that you haven't seen her for the past five months?"

"No."

"Well, you haven't. Arafat invited her to do his biography. She's been on leave in Palestine, following him around. Such a life."

Darrick pointed to the twins. "Maybe you'll have to reconsider how you live your life now."

Dillon turned on him angrily—mostly because that had already occurred to him.

Darrick raised both hands to forestall a retort. "I know," he said quietly. "You don't want to hear it. You hate it when I do that. It just came out instinctively because I spent time with them. I know what it takes. And I also know what it gives you back." He smiled good-naturedly, and changed the subject. "Did you say something about a picnic table when you came in the door? You want me to help you carry it in?"

And so the issue was shelved for the moment. Hamburgers, beans, salads, fruit, cake were handed to Dillon but he passed them on, his appetite gone.

Just as was his anticipation of a month of peace at the beach.

Of course, he had to remember that there was a possibility the babies were Duncan's. No one was sure who they belonged to. Except that it was now established that they weren't Darrick's.

And, if memory served, Duncan had been in Mexico at the time of the twins' conception. That didn't necessarily rule Duncan out as the father, but it probably thinned the chances.

On the other hand, Dillon remembered the desperation with which he and Allison had made love—and felt fairly certain that new life had resulted.

"JUST SIT DOWN," Harper said firmly to Peg and Bertie as they tried to help her clear the picnic table. "Dori and Skye and I can handle this by ourselves."

"Skye's got the baby." Peg fought her for a bowl with just a spoonful of potato salad left. "And you don't know where everything goes."

Harper pulled the bowl out of her grasp. "Neither do you. You haven't been here any longer than I have. Darrick!"

Darrick, holding the other twin, turned away from watching Charlie and Cliff playing rummy on the seat of a lawn chair.

"Come and get your mother," Harper said. "She's interfering with our work."

"Well!" Peg tried to pretend indignation, but was grinning when she allowed her son to lead her away.

Bertie hesitated to stay behind. She whispered, "Peg and I were planning to have margaritas while we cleaned up."

Harper patted her shoulder. "Well, if there's any left when Skye and Dori and I are finished, we'll bring you some."

Bertie folded her arms. "I'd like more reassurance than that."

Skye laughed. "How about if we bring a pitcher right out to you."

"Now you're talking."

Harper led the way indoors with a tottering mountain of dirty bowls and platters. Dori reached around her to open the screen door.

As Harper carried her burden to the kitchen counter, she caught a glimpse of Dillon pacing in the living room, a cell phone to his ear.

"Who's he calling?" Dori asked, putting a stack of paper plates in the trash. "He's supposed to be on vacation."

"I imagine he's trying to find the mother of the twins." Harper spoke casually, as though she really felt as removed from the problem as her behavior this afternoon suggested.

She pretended that nothing had changed between her and the McKeons except that Dillon had come home. She pretended that, despite him she'd held easily to the friendship they'd maintained. But she was putting on a performance that would have done actor Duncan proud.

She didn't know why she should feel so heartbroken. So Dillon had had babies with another woman. She— Harper—was the one who'd walked away from their relationship. And though she couldn't live with him as his wife, she had believed she would always be a part of him, and he of her.

But the twins and their mother—whoever she was— had changed that irrevocably. Now he would belong to *them* heart and soul, no little corner of either left unfilled.

That was how the McKeons were. Family was everything.

Skye came to put an arm around her shoulders, Michelle in her other arm. "Do you know who she is?" she asked gently.

"No, I don't." Harper found herself the subject of Michelle's wide-eyed stare, and grinned. The baby smiled back, gums pink and bare.

"I do," Dori said, coming closer to form a tight little knot with them at the kitchen sink. She looked around to make certain no one had followed them in, and that Dillon was still engrossed in his conversation. Then she focused on Harper. "Do you want to know?" she asked softly.

The mature thing, Harper knew, would have been to say "no." And while she prided herself on her cool and her good sense, they seemed to have fled at the moment. "Yes," she said simply.

Dori leaned closer and said under her breath, "Allison Cartier of CDN. They were in Zaire together. I overheard him telling Darrick when I came down looking for Michelle's pacifier."

Skye's eyes widened like Michelle's. "You mean the TV reporter?"

Dori nodded. "She's probably the only woman in the world who gets to as many crises in as many parts of the world as Dillon does."

Of course, Harper thought. How logical. Dillon and the gorgeous redhead who used to appear regularly on the nightly news—bombs bursting behind her, or fires raging, or riots swelling—were the perfect fit.

Allison Cartier would never ask Dillon to stop running to the latest global hot spot. She would probably simply pack up her babies and follow him, with her own work to do.

Skye gave Harper's shoulders a sympathetic squeeze. "He won't know that the babies are his for certain until he talks to her."

"It doesn't really matter one way or the other," Harper insisted, catching Michelle's hand and leaning over to kiss it. "Of course I want to know the babies will be loved and taken care of, but we can rely on that whichever McKeon they belong to. Dillon himself is of no concern to me."

"Thank you," Dillon said dryly from the doorway. "It's a comfort to know one can be dismissed so easily."

With sisterly disregard for his feelings, Dori ignored his claim and got to the point. "Did you find Allison Cartier?"

He looked surprised.

Dori didn't bother to pretend embarrassment. "I overheard you tell Darrick. I wasn't eavesdropping, I came down to find Michelle's pacifier. Did you find Allison Cartier?"

"No," he replied with a tolerant sigh, apparently resigned to the dearth of privacy. "She was in Palestine working on Arafat's biography, and now she's gone underground with him somewhere. The best I could do was leave a message for her."

"When's she coming back?" Skye asked.

"No one knows. Could be tomorrow, could be a couple of weeks."

Skye shook her head. "And you won't be certain until you find her, will you?"

He inclined his head. "Not absolutely, but I think I know." He went to Skye and looked at the baby at her shoulder. The infant looked back at him. "May I take her? This is Michelle, right?"

"Of course." Skye supported the baby's head and placed her in Dillon's arms.

He handled the baby comfortably, Harper noticed. He was a doctor and therefore used to dealing with them. But it surprised her somewhat that he showed little nervousness, just a very genuine interest.

Skye watched him wander back into the living room with the baby, her eyes wistful.

Harper put a hand to her arm, trying to return a little of the comfort Skye had offered her. "It's going to be hard for you to give them up, isn't it?"

Skye heaved a deep sigh, then seemed determined to accept the fact. "Well," she said with a faint smile, "it'd be harder if they were leaving the family. But Darrick and I will get to see them often."

Dori began loading the dishwasher. "Soon as I get these done, you and I will have to move our things out of Dillon's room, Harper, and move into Duncan's."

"Why don't we just move into yours?" Harper asked. "Don't you have the attic?"

Harper noted that Dori and Skye exchanged a look that was difficult to interpret.

"What?" Harper asked. "Something I don't know?"

Skye ran water in the sink for the pots and pans. "There's a sort of mystery attached to the attic," she said with a measuring look at Harper. "How do you stand on the paranormal?"

Harper blinked. "Ah…I don't think it's come up. I think I'm open to…the possibilities." The direction the conversation was taking suddenly occurred to her and she looked up at Skye in concern. "Unless it's living in the attic. What are we talking about?"

Skye looked around surreptitiously, then smiled. "You want to see?"

Harper turned to Dori for advice. "Do I want to see?"

Dori nodded, closing the dishwasher. "Yeah, I think

so. Come on, I'll help you put those things away, then we'll all go upstairs.''

Several moments later Harper followed with some trepidation as Skye and Dori led the way up the fold-out ladder into the attic.

It was now evening and the room was shadowy, the deep eaves creating pockets of darkness. But right in the middle of the attic, in the dusty light from the window, Skye and Dori had taken posts on either side of an antique dress form. On the upper half was the bodice of a dress in a white silky fabric yellowed with age. It had a ruffled band-collar, and pearls decorating it in a V-pattern starting at the shoulders and ending in a point at the waist. There the fabric was unfinished, threads unraveling, apparently awaiting the attachment of a skirt.

Harper guessed that it had been waiting more than a hundred years.

She went to it, fascinated, wishing she had her camera. In the swirling bar of light from the window, it had an eternal quality she thought she might be able to capture.

She touched the pearls reverently, tracing to the point of the V, then up again. She admired the tiny waist, the nicely rounded bosom above the carefully sewn darts, the puff of the full upper sleeve that narrowed to fit tightly at the wrist.

"Where did you get it?" Harper whispered.

Skye folded her arms, smiling at the bodice. "Well, Darrick and I have a difference of opinion on that. I think it was given to us."

"By whom?"

"By Olivia Marbury."

"Who's she?"

"The woman I think was making the dress."

"I don't understand. Wouldn't she be...dead by now if she was—" Harper stopped, experiencing a sudden little shiver up her spine as she got Skye's point. She looked around the shadowy room. "You mean you think she's..."

Skye, too, looked up into the rafters, her expression more speculative than concerned. "I'm not sure *what* I mean. But Darrick insists the dress form and the mirror weren't here when he and Dillon and Duncan looked at the place. The Realtor doesn't know a thing about it. And Bertie's very familiar with the history of the Buckley family who built this place, and with their family treasures that were moved to a museum in Lincoln City, and *she's* never seen this before."

Harper went to inspect the mirror, an oval cheval glass trimmed in carved oak. "What makes you so sure it belonged to a member of the Buckley family?"

"That's a great story." Skye curled up on the floor cross-legged in front of the form. Dori sat beside her, dusting the base of the form off with her fingertips.

"At the end of the last century," Skye explained, as Harper walked around the standing mirror, "four dancers from San Francisco booked passage on a ship going north, headed for the Klondike."

Harper peered at her from behind the mirror, eyes wide with question. "Looking for gold?"

Skye shrugged. "I suppose looking for steady jobs in a saloon patronized by *men* looking for gold. Anyway, their ship ran up on the rocks off Dancer's Beach—that is, obviously *before* it was Dancer's Beach."

Harper came to sit on the other side of Skye. "So,

that's where the name comes from. Did they all survive?''

Skye smiled. "They did. All saved by three brothers who had a little sawmill here. I love that part of the story."

Harper leaned toward her, elbows on her knees. "Do I detect trouble ahead? Four dancers but only three brothers?"

Skye nodded. "Olivia was a little older than the other girls, and fell in love with the oldest Buckley brother. But he married the youngest of the girls because he wanted a big family and Olivia's health wasn't very strong."

"Makes you wonder why she was going to the Klondike anyway, doesn't it? I mean, if her health was poor." Dori stretched her legs out and leaned back on the flat of her hands.

"Maybe she wanted to be where people wouldn't remind her of that," Harper suggested. "Maybe she just needed adventure whether it was good for her health or not."

Skye beamed at her. "That's what I thought. I believe she was looking for a little excitement in her life and thought she'd found the ultimate adventure when she fell in love with Barton Buckley."

"What did she do when he married someone else?" Harper asked.

"She went on to the Klondike. And twelve years later, when Barton's wife died, guess who went to the Klondike, too?"

"Barton?"

"Precisely."

Harper mulled that over, then looked up at the beautifully beaded silk. "But what makes you think this dress was going to be hers? Barton did marry someone else.''

''He did. But he and Olivia kept company for a time before that, and I think she believed they were going to be married and worked on this dress. Probably even privately, never telling anyone, just holding the dream close. Until he found out she was ill.''

''Where has it been all this time?''

''I don't know.''

''Well, why would it be here if she went to the Klondike? Do you think she left it?''

''She might have, but she did come back.'' Skye tucked a wayward strand of dark hair behind her ear. ''I've been researching her and found a reference to an aunt in a cookbook written by a Buckley daughter-in-law. It related to a recipe for chicken soup. She said an old aunt who was staying with them swore by it to relieve the croup.''

''And you think that the old aunt was Olivia returned? You think Barton found her and brought her back?''

''I haven't found positive evidence of it, but I'd like to think that's what happened.''

''But the guys said the bodice wasn't here when they looked at the house.''

''Right.''

''You mean it just...appeared?''

''I think so.''

''Why?''

Skye smiled. ''I have a theory on that.''

Dori leaned behind Skye to warn Harper in a loud whisper, ''Brace yourself.''

Skye warned Dori into silence with a look, then contemplated the pearls on the bodice that were catching the lowering sunlight. "At first I thought she'd brought it for me," she said. "Because I wasn't sure for a while there that Darrick and I could make a life together. But finding the bodice filled me with hope." She turned to Harper as though to judge whether or not she understood.

Harper didn't—at least not entirely—but she'd always loved a mystery, and certainly a mystery about star-crossed lovers given a second chance was more intriguing than most.

Skye gestured toward the bodice. "It represents Olivia's hopes and dreams, and helped me keep mine alive when I was sure they were lost." She nodded as though she'd reached some previously unclear conclusion. "But now I think it wasn't meant for me exclusively. Maybe it was a gift to the house. I think it's here to help you, too."

Harper stared at her. "Me?"

"You," Skye affirmed, then added carefully, "and Dillon."

Harper shook her head. "There's me, and there's Dillon, but there's no 'me and Dillon.'" She tried to rise, but Skye stopped her with a hand on her arm.

"Maybe there should be."

Harper studied her new friend in fond exasperation, then said slowly, clearly, "He had twins with another woman, Skye. So what there *should* be is Dillon and Allison What's-her-name."

"We don't know that for certain."

"He seems to be certain."

Skye raised a shoulder in a gesture that suggested there were no certainties. "Darrick was sure the twins were *his*." She smiled. "I think a man looks at those beautiful babies and wants to take credit for them."

"Oh, no."

All three women turned at the sound of the male voice.

Darrick stood on the ladder, head and shoulders rising from the trap. He shook his head over the semicircle of women at the base of the dress form.

"Skye, what are you doing?" he asked with a note of forbearance. "Tell me you're not scaring Harper and Dori with tales of ghostly Olivia."

"It's not scary," Dori denied. "It's sweet and romantic."

"Oh, right," he said. "I can see it now. The first night you spend up here alone, you'll be asking for a night-light, then wanting me to check the closet every twenty minutes."

Dori made a face at him. "There is no closet. And Harper and I are sleeping up here tonight just to prove you wrong."

He looked around with a frown, as though he hadn't previously noticed the absence of a closet. "Oh, yeah. I guess we'll have to do something about that."

"I'm going home tonight," Harper reminded Dori.

"I thought the cabs were down."

"Only one of them's down. The other took a fare to Portland. He should be back by now."

"I just called for you," Darrick said. "He isn't back. Apparently there's heavy holiday traffic on Highway 18."

Harper met his gaze and held it, not entirely sure she believed him.

He didn't flinch.

She resigned herself to staying the night. Whether up here with Skye's ghost or downstairs with the ghosts of her past with Dillon didn't make much difference.

"Mom's taking a poll for video rentals," Darrick said, refocusing on the women, "and Dad's setting up for gin rummy." He pointed to Harper. "He said you weren't allowed to play."

She laughed and got to her feet. "That's because he's still into me for fifteen bucks from the *last* game. We'll see who's allowed to play and who isn't."

They all paraded down the ladder. In the kitchen, Peg and Bertie were making fresh coffee, filling the tea kettle, putting cookies on a plate.

In the living room where Charlie and Cliff were opening out a card table, Dillon sat on the loveseat with a baby in each arm, staring at them with a small mysterious frown.

Harper found the picture both touching and unsettling. If he knew what she knew...

Chapter Three

Dillon insisted on keeping the twins in his room that night.

"They're up a couple of times before morning," Skye said, trying to convince him to let her and Darrick keep them. "You just got back from Nicaragua. Let them stay with us. We'll be going home day after tomorrow, then you'll have to deal with them on your own. Take a break while you can."

He shook his head. "Thanks, but you've been dealing with a responsibility that's really mine, so I'll take over now. As a doctor, I've had more experience with babies than you realize."

"For forty-five minutes or an hour at a time," Darrick countered. "It's a little different twenty-four hours a day. By next week, a night on the rack will seem like a vacation."

"I'll be fine," Dillon assured him. He had to be, he thought. Darrick always took up everybody's slack. He'd helped Dillon pass chemistry in high school, he'd lent him money in college, he'd bullied suppliers into advancing him equipment when he opened the clinic.

Dillon appreciated Darrick, but seeing to his own children was something he had to do himself. Just under the surface of his confidence was stark terror. But this was something he had to do.

"Well...call us if you need us," Skye said doubtfully. "We're just down the hall."

"I feel guilty," Peg said, "that your father and I have this beautifully furnished room and you kids are sleeping in sleeping bags."

"I don't," Charlie said. "After all our kids have put us through, we deserve to be comfortable."

Darrick, Dori and Dillon expelled simultaneous gasps of indignation.

"I was exemplary!"

"All your friends said we were model children!"

"Everything was Duncan's fault!"

The last came from Dillon, who hurried to defend his claim when his siblings turned to look at him. "Well, it was. He was such a good actor, even then, that he could be smiling with blueberries in his teeth and blame us for eating the pie."

Darrick nodded. "I remember that incident. Only you got off scot-free because you were the 'baby,' and Duncan was so convincing no one believed he did it—so that left me."

Peg frowned. "You *did* do it."

He pretended hurt feelings. "I know. And I shared with everybody like you taught me. But it wasn't fair to suspect me first."

Skye pulled him toward the stairs. "I think we'd better get to bed before you talk yourself into some other crime."

Hugs were given, good-nights were called. Dori walked Dillon up the stairs, Harper trailing behind them.

"Don't worry about a thing," Dori said, patting his back. "I'm an excellent nanny."

"So Darrick told me." He did his best to keep the pleading out of his voice. "Are you willing to stay on?"

"Of course. Provided you pay me well and treat me fairly."

"There you go making demands already."

"But I can't start right away."

Now he had to keep the panic out of his voice. "Why not?"

"Because I have to go back to Edenfield for a couple of days. I've been invited to speak to the Jane Austen Society on Wednesday and I don't have a thing prepared yet. I can be here Thursday, though."

Thursday! Two and a half days alone! "Great," he lied.

IT WAS BARELY TWO A.M. when he realized that being a parent was considerably different from being a doctor. Whatever skill he had as a physician didn't seem to apply here.

He handled the babies comfortably because he was accustomed to that, but there'd always been a waiting mother's arms in which to put them when he'd finished what he had to do.

This time there was no handing them off. He was it.

When he finally got both babies to sleep again at the same time at 2:30, he called CDN to see if they'd heard from Allison yet. They hadn't. He was tempted to go to Palestine himself to retrieve her.

He put his cell phone in one of his shoes placed side by side near his sleeping bag, and eased his tense muscles into the soft down. He drew a deep breath and groaned quietly.

One of the twins woke up screaming.

Dillon kicked at the zipped-up bag that confined him, scrambled to his knees and reached the crib in three long strides. He lifted the baby into his arms before she could wake her sister and went to the farthest end of the room, bouncing and shushing her.

Just half an hour ago he'd fed and changed both babies. He'd often told worried mothers with the same complaint, who'd had their babies tested for every problem known to medicine, that it was probably some indefinable something that wasn't life-threatening, but that the baby was unable to express in any other way than crying.

He hadn't realized until this moment what scant comfort that advice was.

His bedroom door opened softly. He peered through the darkness and saw a short shape moving, closing the door.

"Dori?" he asked.

"Harper," came the quiet reply. "Michelle likes me. I thought I might be able to help."

Of all the questions he might have asked at that moment, the one that came out was, "How do you know it's Michelle?"

"Her voice is a little higher, a little more desperate." Fingers brushed his arm and the baby was taken from him. He stood quietly as a current seemed to run through him, as though he'd stuck a fork in a toaster. "Skye insists Michelle is going to be an artist or a ballerina. She seems to be all nerves and emotion."

Harper paced as she spoke, all sign of the antagonistic woman he'd dealt with that afternoon gone as she concentrated on the baby. Of course, Dillon thought grimly, babies, a picket fence and a rose garden were all she'd ever wanted.

"How do you know all that?" he asked. "I didn't realize you'd been around the babies that much."

"Instinctive, I guess," she replied, concentrating on the baby. "And Michelle and I have bonded. She's sort of adrift, like I was. Only she's going from one father to another instead of from one aunt to another."

Harper's aunts were wonderful, but Dillon knew enough about her childhood to know that their globe-trotting life-styles had been hard on her—prompting a desperate search for security after the death of her parents.

"How *are* the aunts?" he asked. As he recalled, the one-time singing group had diversified. One aunt was now an agent, one a writer, two of them still had a nightclub act, and one did voice-overs for animated films.

"Good," she replied in a whisper, as Michelle began to settle down. The whisper required that she come closer to him to reply. "But Aunt Phyl just had knee replacement surgery. That's why I was in Edenfield and not in Seattle. I was supposed to nurse her through an 'invalid' period, but since then she's had all kinds of company, is driving the shopping networks crazy, and is now being visited by Aunt Aggie. So Peg invited me to come here for the weekend."

"Lucky for Michelle," he said.

She was close enough that he could smell the lily-of-the-valley scent she always wore. It had clung to the pillowcase long after she had left him. The first night without her, he'd thrown the pillow across the room, then in the early morning had retrieved it and had kept it beside him ever since as a sort of exquisite torture. It reminded him of a lesson he'd learned very early in life—that not everything you loved had staying power.

"Are you still tied up with Wade 'Wacko' Wienermeier?" he asked, the invasion of his memories creating a sudden tension.

He felt the answering tension in her as she hesitated. "I'm still in partnership with Wade—Warren—Winthrop." She enunciated the triple-barreled name clearly, carefully. "We've gone into a little advertising photography on the side that's turning out to be a bigger part of the business than we anticipated."

"And you trust him to keep everything going while you're away?"

"He's very capable and extremely competent."

"When he's not outrunning an irate husband...or dating triplets."

"The woman *told* him she was single," she replied, her voice quiet but ripe with irritation, "and the triplets were an assignment."

"The *Kama Sutra* comes with a workbook now?"

There was a long silence, then he heard low, crooning from the crib. That was followed by the sound of his bedroom door opening and closing.

He was alone.

As his brain formed that thought, his heart grasped the full import of the words and realized they applied to more than just the moment.

Then there was a small, sweet baby sound from the crib. He tensed, expecting it to be followed by a demanding wail. But a contented silence followed.

Well. A little glow in his chest elbowed aside the terrors of his new fatherhood. He wasn't *entirely* alone.

HARPER AWOKE TO THE PATTER OF RAIN against the attic window. Dori's sleeping bag was empty, and there was a stillness in the room that stirred Harper's imagination.

She sat up, half expecting to find the bodice and the mirror gone, a figment of the lively imaginations of three susceptible young women.

But it was there, shining and lovely in the early morning light. It was so delicate, so elegantly beaded, so graceful of line that her mind created an image of the wearer.

She would have been a little taller than Harper, but with a tiny waist usually only made possible by a good corset. A brunette, Harper imagined, because she'd always thought them more dramatic than blondes, and Olivia's certainly was a dramatic story. She'd have had large dark eyes with a sad look in them, and possibly a pale complexion because her health had been fragile.

Then Harper's mind put Olivia in the bodice, added a white taffeta skirt with matching beading along the hem, and sent her down the aisle of a little country church toward the eldest Buckley brother waiting near the altar rail.

The smallest sigh of a breeze blew through the room and the pointed sleeve of the bodice fluttered.

The pointed sleeve of the bodice fluttered!

Harper stared, unable to move.

Because there was nothing to cause a breeze. The window was latched, the trap door was closed. Nothing had moved.

Except the sleeve of the dress.

My mind did that, she told herself. *I was imagining her walking up the aisle in the bodice. I just carried it*

*a step further and imagined her raising her hand to
her groom. That was it.*

Heart pounding, Harper scrambled out of the bag,
snatched up her jeans and shirt and yanked open the
trap door. She literally ran down the ladder as goose-
flesh broke out on her arms.

She missed a rung near the bottom and let out a little
cry of distress as she held tightly to an upper rung with
her hand, her clothes still clutched in her other arm.

Something with steel muscle snaked around her
waist from behind and tipped her slightly backward.

"I've got you," Dillon said, a subtle edge of mockery to his voice. "You can let go."

Dillon. There was something instantly stabilizing
about his presence. It brought her back to reality with
a thud.

He set her on her feet and turned her around, holding
her arms while he looked into her face.

"What?" he asked, a pleat forming between his eyebrows.

A little of the eeriness clung to her as though she'd
been snagged in a very fine net. "Nothing," she said
with a gusty breath. "I just... Nothing."

One of his hands unconsciously caressed her arm in
a comforting gesture. It took all her willpower not to
lean into it.

"You're pale." He put a knuckle to her cheek and
his frown deepened. "Your lip's trembling. What
frightened you?"

She *was* trembling, but that was *his* fault. For a
woman who'd done fine without him for almost two
years, she was disheartened to discover that one touch
flamed all the old lust back to roaring life again.

If she gave him the opportunity to laugh at her, it

would refresh all her old grievances and bring sanity back.

"Do you know about Olivia?" she asked.

He smiled, but without derision. "Skye's ghost? Yes, she was telling me about it just now over coffee." His eyes swung from her to the open trap, then back to her again. "Did you...see her?"

"No." She shifted her clothes to her other arm and her weight from one foot to the other. "I...think I probably just wasn't quite awake and..." She hesitated, looking up at him from under her eyelashes, certain that her next admission would bring a scornful laugh. She squared her shoulders and took a breath. "I thought I saw something move, that's all. But like I said, I was just waking up and I...I..."

No laugh. No scorn. "What moved?" he asked seriously.

A little off balance, she admitted too much. "The sleeve of the bodice. But I think it was because I was imagining her in it, walking down the aisle, and..."

That was what finally did it. There was no mockery in his eyes over what she said she'd experienced, but her mention of walking down the aisle caused a subtle change in his expression. She caught it instantly.

And suddenly, just as she'd predicted, all the old grievances were back. She remembered why she'd been unable to stay with him.

"Take it easy," she said, taking two steps back out of his reach. "You weren't in the picture. Your precious freedom is secure."

Temper flared in his dark eyes. "I might have enjoyed being married to Olivia," he said, the line of his jaw square and tight. "A nice old-fashioned girl taught to make *polite* conversation."

She rolled her eyes, her tension dissipating as anger broke free. ''In your opinion, a woman shows good manners only when she agrees with you, only when she dismisses what *she* wants, to see that you get what *you* want.''

That finally elicited the mockery. ''Then you never displayed good manners with me, did you? Our entire relationship was based on you trying to push out of our lives everything I wanted.''

''What you want isn't healthy!''

''I'm a doctor! I know more about what's healthy than you do!''

''You're an emotional quadriplegic!''

''And you're an osteoporotic spur on my coccyx!''

She'd been around his doctor-talk long enough to know he'd just called her a pain in the butt. She turned in indignation, headed for the bathroom, but found the door closed. She stopped uncertainly in the middle of the corridor, unwilling to go downstairs in the long T-shirt she'd worn to bed, but determined not to return into the attic—at least for now.

Dillon held a hand out toward the open door of his room. ''Please,'' he said with exaggerated politeness. ''Use my bathroom. May I stay to hold your head under?''

She stormed past him through the bedroom and into the bathroom, and slammed the door.

''WE ALL PICK a redecorating chore that can be done this afternoon,'' Peg explained after lunch, ''to do our part for the house. Then we'll have Skye's lasagne and salad for dinner, and watch Duncan's movie as our last hurrah before we all go home tomorrow.'' She placed a list in the middle of the table. ''Your father jotted down some of the jobs that can be done in a couple of hours.''

Darrick, sitting next to Charlie, elbowed him teasingly. ''So I guess you get out of a job because you made the contribution of preparing the list.''

''No such luck,'' he replied. ''Your mother's already assigned me to paint the kitchen table and chairs.''

Darrick studied the list. ''I thought you outranked her?''

Charlie laughed mirthlessly. ''What galaxy are you from, Pilgrim?''

The group at the table burst into laughter. Peg withstood it with a dignified tilt of her chin. ''Someone has to organize this motley crew into an efficient force.''

''We're not going to war, Mom,'' Dillon said, taking the list from Darrick. ''We're just working on a house. I'll wash the windows.'' He passed the list back to Darrick.

''New bathroom faucets.'' Darrick said.

Skye looked over his shoulder. ''Um...wallpaper border in the kitchen.'' She looked up at Peg in surprise. ''We have some?''

''Dad and I picked some up at a sidewalk sale. You said you painted everything white, so anything will go with it.''

''What did you buy?'' Darrick asked after a concerned look at Dillon.

''It's a long row of canned fruit and vegetable labels. Very colorful. You'll love it. Dori, you'll have to watch the babies for Dill. Harper, what do you want to do?''

Harper took the list from Darrick. The unclaimed jobs included water-sealing the front porch, putting up curtain rods, hanging mini-blinds and installing floor covering on the sunporch.

"The floor covering is Cliff and Bertie's contribution," Charlie said. "They used to be in the business."

"That's generous," Darrick said. "Thank you."

Cliff nodded modestly. "Least we can do. We intend to come and visit often. That is, if Dillon doesn't mind, since he'll be in residence now."

Dillon shook his head. "Of course not. That's what beach houses are all about—open air, lots of naps and constant company."

"Speaking of naps," Darrick said, "you have to check out the hammock." Then he cast a scolding glance at Harper. "But not when she's around. She and Dori and Skye dumped me out of it."

"Only because you deserved it." Harper handed the list back to Peg with a teasing grin. "I'll hang the curtain rods. Looks like that leaves you with water-sealing the front porch and installing mini-blinds."

Peg reached across the table to pat her cheek. "Aren't you cute. I'll charm the men into doing it for me. You see, if you were from the old school like me, rather than a young upstart like yourself who is above tricks and games, you, too, could get a man to do the hard things for you."

Harper smiled and tried to look as though she really *was* above those things. "But what would that prove to me about myself?"

Peg appeared surprised by the question. "That you're smart enough to get out of doing what you'd rather not do."

"You had to ask," Skye laughed, shaking her head at Harper.

THE BIG HOUSE was filled with the sound of drilling, hammering, spraying, laughing and, occasionally, swearing. Everyone concentrated on his or her assigned task in the spirit of a family project.

In an hour and a half, Harper had installed all the spindle-tipped rods on the downstairs windows, and had moved upstairs.

She dragged her short wooden ladder into Dillon's room, carefully walked around his sleeping bag and a tidy pile of clothes, and set the ladder up in front of the window.

She climbed atop it, tape measure and pencil in hand, and found herself face to face with Dillon. For an instant this so surprised her that she tottered and had to grasp the window frame for support.

Of course, she remembered. He was washing windows.

He made an instinctive gesture to reach for her, but the obstruction of the window prevented him. He knocked on the glass and made a ''raise the window'' gesture with his right hand.

Making sure his hands were clear, she unlocked the old knob fastener and pushed on the upper part of the frame. The window slid up and she stepped down a rung to peer out at him. ''Yeah?'' she asked.

''Are you up to doing that?'' he asked, leaning over to look in at her.

''The downstairs is already done.'' Her tone was superior. ''I'll probably finish before you, and all you're doing is washing.''

He ignored the implied criticism. ''I mean, are you competent to use a ladder. This morning you fell halfway down the attic ladder.''

''I didn't fall,'' she corrected, ''I was holding on. You're the one who pulled me off.''

''Because your feet were dangling.''

"I was…"

To her surprise, he smiled suddenly—a sweet smile she remembered from the old days. "I know," he said indulgently. "You'd seen a ghost."

She gave him a mildly punitive look. "This morning you were nice enough not to laugh at me."

He shook his head. "I'm not laughing. I just think it's interesting that a woman who's always so sure of everything can believe in something as inexplicable as a ghost."

"I didn't say I believed."

"You ran from it. You must have believed."

She sighed, reaching up for the bottom of the raised window. "Move your hands off the sill before I close this on them," she warned.

He didn't move, except to step one rung down so that he didn't have to lean over to look at her. And he was still smiling. "Wimpy Wade make you so tough?"

That was all it took to make her want to punch him in the nose. "He isn't wimpy, and I'm not tough. You just bring out my defensive side."

"Why do you suppose that is?"

"Because you're generally impossible." She made as though to close the window again. "Would you move your hands, please?"

Instead of cooperating, he placed the short-handled squeegee on the ladder's shelf, and leaned his elbows on the windowsill. His eyes looked into hers as though trying to analyze her.

"I remember," he said quietly, "when you thought I was pretty great."

"We all have our delusions. If we're going to fin—"

"I thought *you* were pretty great," he interrupted.

Then his eyes perused her face, moving from feature to feature as though she were brand new to him.

Her breath began to come in gasps. "But not great enough to...to spend a lifetime with."

He sighed quietly. The exhalation seemed to indicate tolerance rather than annoyance. "You're always so into defining everything—telling me what it must or mustn't be."

"I would think that'd make sense to a doctor. How can you treat something if you haven't diagnosed it, determined what it is?"

He leaned a little closer. "Love's not an illness, Harper," he said. "It's supposed to be an adventure."

"You can't run through love blindly," she insisted, distracted by the nearness of his mouth. "It's all very...complicated."

He considered that, and her. Then he reached through the open window, caught the back of her head in his hand, and drew her toward him. "Let me simplify it for you," he whispered, his eyes on her mouth.

She parted her lips to protest what she knew was coming, but she was too late. His mouth was already on hers, and it was all so deliciously familiar and, despite her attempts to convince herself otherwise, so longed-for, that she slipped into the spell.

She'd always thought him a wonderful kisser. He was never hesitant, never awkward, never halfhearted. His hands were firm and sure, his lips skilful, even inspired. In the time they'd been apart she hadn't forgotten what it felt like to be touched—or kissed—by him.

But now as she experienced it again, it was as though her perception had expanded—or the world had shrunk. His impact was large, deep, more powerful than her recollection. Her lips tingled with the warm impression of his, her ears rang with the sudden rise in blood pressure, her knees felt weak as his tongue traced a tender circle just inside her lips.

Then he drew back. "Why would you ever want to tie that down to fit some schedule that only serves to confine everyone else?"

It wasn't until he posed the question that she was able to struggle back to her senses. Damn it. It was depressing to know how easily she'd fallen for his line when she knew better—had known better for a long time.

"Because love isn't just for your pleasure," she said quietly, angrily. "It's supposed to serve a purpose, to be put to use. Not simply to be played with. Now, move your hands—or lose them."

She slammed the window down.

He pulled away just in time.

Chapter Four

They watched *Gone Before Morning* on video after dinner. It was the story of a middle-class housewife who was neglected by her husband, and who took up with the friend of a wealthy college classmate while both were summer houseguests.

Duncan McKeon played the man with whom the housewife was indiscreet.

Harper had met Duncan only once, several Christmases before, and she'd found him witty, charming and devastatingly handsome. She'd thought it fascinating that he'd built a superlative career playing the villain, when he was such a nice man.

His brothers assured her that he wasn't the paragon he pretended to be to friends and acquaintances: he was stubborn and had a temper and an annoying preference for martial music. But all the brothers were always harassing or playfully insulting one another, and so she didn't believe them for a moment.

But as she watched his character unfold on the screen she thought it remarkable that he could so transform himself. From the amiable companion he initially seemed to be, he turned into a cunning opportunist who'd mistaken the housewife for a woman of means whom he intended to use for his own ends. It was insidious the way he made his charm and good looks work for him.

His flawless features, his seemingly artless wit, his devastating smile—all added a dimension to his selfish machinations that deepened his villainy, yet made the viewer hope for his redemption.

When it failed to come and the housewife went home to her husband, her pain was palpable to the audience because they, too, had wanted more from him.

After the final credits rolled, there was a brief feature on how the film was made, and interviews with the principal characters.

When asked how he prepared for his role of villain time after time, Duncan—wearing a white sweater that seemed to magnify his good looks while he relaxed in a director's chair—replied that it was no different from preparing to play a hero.

"A villain is just a hero turned inside out," he said. "He's equipped with all the qualities that could have made him a hero, except that he uses them for an evil or selfish purpose."

There was a moment's silence among the family.

Dillon turned to Darrick. "When did he become so profound?"

"I don't know," Darrick replied with a frown. "Scary, isn't it? I suppose that means he won't be up for our beer and brot fest on the Fourth of July?"

"I wouldn't jump to conclusions," Charlie said as he aimed the clicker at the VCR and rewound the tape. "He's good at what he does because he thinks deeply about it. But at heart, he'll always be our Duncan."

"But right now," Peg said with sudden briskness as

she sat forward in her chair and took in the group gathered there, "we have to think about Dillon."

Even Dillon looked at her in surprise. "Why?" he asked.

"Because you won't be able to handle the twins by yourself until Dori gets back," she said, a hand, palm upward, stabbing the air as though that should be obvious. "But Darrick's due back at work, Skye has to set up business in Edenfield, and Dad and I are leaving Wednesday morning for a week in Palm Springs with a seniors' tour. We won't even get home from there until the following Wednesday."

Darrick leaned back in his chair and grinned at his parents. "Why do you have a house anyway? You're such a pair of vagabonds. All you really need are two camels and a couple of burnooses."

Dori leaned over the coffee table that held snacks, and scooped up sour cream and salsa with the corner of a tortilla chip. "Burnooses?"

"The robes they wear," he clarified.

"The camels?" Dillon asked innocently.

Darrick sent him a quelling look. "The Arabs who ride the camels."

Peg shook her head at Harper. "Trying to keep this group on track has made me old before my time."

Charlie laughed and patted her knee affectionately. "Oh, come on, Peggy. It *is* time." Then he looked around the room. "What she's trying to say is that someone has to stay with Dillon, and none of us can." His gaze stopped on Harper. "What about you, Harper? Your aunt's going to be on that cruise for another week, isn't she?"

Trapped, Harper thought. She looked into Charlie's seemingly guileless gaze. She was, she realized, locked as securely as Houdini in his chains underwater in the glass box.

And perhaps about to suffer the same fate.

No. She couldn't. She wouldn't. She'd spill her guts and be in a worse mess than she was now.

She fought valiantly. "I intended to go back to my studio and get a head start on a new advertising campaign we've taken on."

"No kidding." Darrick leaned toward her interestedly. "For whom?"

Peg had been right about keeping this group on track, Harper thought.

"Manchester Linens," she replied. "And I'd real—"

"Manchester Linens—" Skye frowned in thought, then snapped her fingers "—the people who claim their bedding is 'nursery soft'! Harper!" She indicated the babies asleep in their carrier at Dillon's feet. "Your campaign is made right there."

"You're right!" Peg shrieked.

The family took up the cry, ignoring her completely as they told each other how perfect Michelle and Gabrielle would be for such a campaign.

Harper put a hand to her eyes.

Dillon whistled everyone into silence. When they all turned to him in surprise, his glance grazed over Harper and he said calmly, "You're forgetting one very important thing. I don't want her here." He focused on his mother, his eyes scolding. "You don't think you're fooling anybody, do you, Mom? You want us back together, but it isn't going to happen. We broke up for good reasons both of us still believe in, so please give it up."

Dillon spoke without heat. But his brutally frank

words hung in the air while his mother looked at him as though she would still make him pay for bad manners.

He knew he'd have a tough time dealing with the twins alone. And though Harper still annoyed the hell out of him, he had feelings for her he hadn't been able to shake. They'd billowed and almost overwhelmed him yesterday when he walked into the kitchen and saw her standing there.

Dear God, he thought. Could he have gotten himself into a *bigger* mess? Could he have made his future any more complicated?

If he was going to straighten things out, Harper *had* to stay. And he could think of no more sure way to make that happen than to let her believe he was insisting that she go.

He *had* to achieve some kind of closure with her—particularly now that he'd fathered another woman's babies.

Harper met his eyes across the silent, watchful group. "Do you mind if I make a long-distance call to Seattle?" she asked tightly.

"Yes," he replied.

Ignoring him, she stood and went to the kitchen. She was back in a moment, her expression grim. "I can stay," she said.

"I don't want you to stay," he pushed.

"I didn't say *I* wanted to stay," she said in a tone he thought of as a sweet snarl, "I just said I can."

"I'll be back as quickly as possible," Dori assured him.

He pretended to be disgruntled. "Great."

The women carried the snack bowls into the kitchen,

and his father and Cliff moved the collection of chairs back to their respective rooms.

Darrick caught Dillon's arm and pulled him out onto the front porch. "Good performance," he said as he closed the door behind him.

Dillon could have asked him what he meant, but there was no point. Darrick had always been able to see through him. "I thought so," he said instead. He went halfway down the steps, then sat on one, leaning his elbows back on an upper stair.

"You're still in love with her." Darrick sat just above him and leaned back against the baluster.

"I don't know."

"You're going to have to decide."

Dillon gave his brother a dry glance. "Thank you, oh great guru of personal relationships. I didn't know that."

"What are you going to do?"

"I'm going to spend a month learning to care for my daughters," Dillon said. "I'm going to try to find their mother, and try to figure out how Harper feels about me."

"I thought the kiss in the open window was pretty telling."

Dillon turned in irritation. "How'd you know about that?"

"I was putting new faucets in the bathroom across the hall. The mirror on the medicine cabinet lines up with your bedroom window. And in case you were too carried away to notice, you weren't the only one into that kiss."

"Yeah, well..." Dillon faced the front yard again with a sigh. "Even when she loves me, she hates me. We've got kind of a strange thing going. I didn't entirely understand it even when it was going well. The woman's perverse.''

Darrick laughed softly. ''It's a quality they all share.'' There was a moment's pause. Dillon smiled into the twilight, knowing what was coming. ''You going to be all right?''

''Of course,'' he replied.

''If you need me, just call. I can be here in an hour and a half.''

''Provided I wanted you here.''

''Don't be smug, Dill,'' Darrick said amiably. ''You're going to be dealing with two babies and a woman at the same time. Before the month is out you're going to need Freud himself to keep you sane.''

Dillon turned to look at him again. ''Skye seems like an angel.''

Darrick smiled slowly. ''She is. But she can be a little devil, too. That's *another* quality they all share.''

Dillon arched an eyebrow. ''Are *you* going to be okay?''

''A-1,'' Darrick replied. ''The difference is, I know that I love her and that she loves me. And I know why. You're still in doubt.''

Dillon rolled his eyes, then focused them on the sky once again. ''Harper makes natural disasters seem easy.''

''Welcome home.''

THE HOUSE WAS EMPTY far too quickly. Darrick and Dillon went to the bank together the following morning, while Cliff and Charlie dropped the trailer at the U-Haul dealer in town, and Bertie helped Peg pack the motor home.

Harper and Dori tactfully left a tearful Skye alone with the babies.

"I'm sure she'd be back here in a flash," Dori said to Harper with a thin smile, "if you get to the point where you need a break." They were in the attic packing up Dori's single suitcase.

"Oh, you'll be back in a couple of days." Harper handed her a balled pair of socks that had rolled away.

"When Michelle won't stop crying, a couple of minutes can seem like an eternity."

"I'll be fine." Harper caught Dori's arm so she was forced to look at her. "Just don't forget that this is your job and not mine. I'll expect you on Thursday."

Dori put her hand over Harper's. "Are you going to make up with Dillon?"

Harper swatted the arm she'd held. "Didn't you hear what he said? He doesn't want me here. And I don't want to be here. I'm just trying to help the twins."

"He doesn't want you here," Dori said, pulling the lid down on the case and snapping it closed, "because he thinks you don't want to be here."

"Well, he's right."

"Come on. It's me—Dori. You can tell me the truth."

Harper sighed. "We don't want the same things, Dori. And now he's had babies with another woman. Even if it were possible to work out our differences, he should live his life with her, not with me."

"We don't know for certain that she's the mother."

"He seems to think she is."

"He might be wrong."

"Well, don't say that so he can hear you. It'll offend his messianic complex."

To Harper's chagrin, Dori looked affronted rather

than amused. In their easy conversation, Harper had forgotten that one never disparaged Dori's brothers in front of her.

"He doesn't help out of ego," she said a trifle coolly. "He takes his oath seriously. I'm surprised that you could have lived with him and not know that."

"I do know that," Harper replied, regretting that she'd upset Dori, but knowing a truth Dori didn't understand. "But sometimes I think he uses it as an escape from his everyday life."

Dori got to her feet and picked up her bag. Harper stood, too.

Dori went to the bodice and took the beaded tip of the sleeve in the fingers of her free hand. It was the same sleeve Harper had thought she'd seen move yesterday.

Harper's heart bumped against her ribs.

"Are you going to continue to check out Olivia?" Dori asked.

Skye had extracted that promise from her this morning over breakfast. "I'll do what I can. How do you think this got here?"

Dori dropped the sleeve and studied the bodice one more moment. "I haven't a clue. But it's a nice thought, isn't it? That someone from…beyond, has come back to the place where she was in love to help other people in love."

Harper had to admit that it was—even if the whole thing still felt a little spooky. If anyone needed otherworldly help, it was she.

Then the men returned and the motor home was packed. Before long, the senior McKeons were on their way, an arm waving out of each side of the vehicle.

"I'm really going to miss them," Bertie said

heavily. The Fishers and the McKeons had become fast friends over the long weekend.

"Then you'll have to come and see us a lot," Dillon said, patting Bertie's shoulder. "You're always welcome."

"We're glad to have you here," Cliff said.

When the Fishers returned home, Darrick and Skye packed the Lexus. Then they held the twins for several minutes, saying their goodbyes.

Harper, her throat burning because of the tears in Skye's eyes, saw the distress on Dillon's face.

"Harper will send you pictures," he said, hugging Skye as she handed him Gabrielle. "And you guys'll be coming all the time. I'll take good care of them, I swear."

"I know you will." Skye forced a smile, then turned quickly and hurried out the door.

With a concerned glance after her, Darrick gave Michelle a final hug, then passed her to Harper.

"God, I'm sorry," Dillon said fervently.

Darrick wrapped him in a hug, careful of the baby he held. "It's all right. It'll just take us a while to adjust. Take care. No, don't come out to the car." He put a hand to Dillon's shoulder. "It'll be easier this way. But we'll see you for the Fourth."

"Right."

Darrick smiled at Harper. "Bye."

Her reply was high and unsteady. "Bye, Darrick."

The front door closed behind him, and Dillon and Harper both stared at it until they heard the sound of the Lexus backing out of the driveway. Then the white car passed the front window, headed for Edenfield.

"Hell," Dillon said grimly.

"Yeah," Harper agreed.

But they were left with little time to commiserate over Darrick and Skye's loss. Both babies began to fuss the moment the Lexus disappeared, almost as though they knew Dillon and Harper were the B team. And, as usually happened, Michelle's whimpers swelled quickly into screams of distress.

Harper, holding her, began a frantic search for a pacifier.

"Skye put them in a plastic cup on the counter," Dillon told her, bouncing Gabrielle as she fussed halfheartedly. "They're probably hungry already. I'll get bottles ready."

They met at the loveseat a few moments later. Dillon held two bottles trapped in the fingers of his left hand.

Harper took one and settled onto the left side of the loveseat, making room for him to join her. He chose instead to occupy the Boston rocker his father had left in a corner.

Gabrielle began to eat greedily. Michelle screamed against the removal of the pacifier, then quieted magically when Harper put the nipple into her mouth.

"Do you want to talk about how we're going to do this?" Dillon asked, gently rocking. He hadn't intended his tone to be defensive, but he knew it was.

Harper gave him a look that suggested disinterest. "I believe it's completely covered in Dr. Spock."

"I don't mean the babies. I mean us."

"I thought we covered this. We're not us. We're you and me. And the house is big enough that we won't be continually bumping into each other."

"That might work if we weren't caring for twins. They need to be together. Therefore, *we* have to spend some time together."

She looked at him, her jaw set. Then it softened as

she appeared to consider that. "Okay," she said finally. "I think the only thing that'll work is to decide here and now that all we talk about are the babies and the house."

Dillon felt a surge of resentment. She was always setting down the rules. Of course, he had foolishly asked her the question: he shouldn't be surprised that her answer was legislative.

"I don't agree," he said quietly, but with an authority he considered rightfully his as the father of the babies and one of the owners of the house. "*I* have the maturity to discuss things on which we disagree. Don't you?"

She closed her eyes. "Dillon, you're starting already and we've been alone all of fifteen minutes." She heaved a sigh suggestive of strained patience. "You said you didn't want me here, and you know I don't want to be here. So let's just do whatever it takes to coexist until Thursday."

"I said I didn't want you here because I didn't think you'd want to stay." That ploy had worked well, but he was careful not to let his satisfaction show. "You're the one who insisted. So what am I to take from that?"

"Nothing," she said a little hotly. "Nothing, Dill. It doesn't mean I harbor old feelings for you, or that I'd like to resurrect them, or...or...anything! It means I stayed because I knew you'd need help with the babies, and I've grown fond of them. That's *all.*"

Gabrielle stopped eating to draw breath. Dillon put her to his shoulder and patted her gently, questioning Harper's statement with a quirk of his eyebrow.

"You think I'm lying to you?" she asked wearily.

"I think you're lying to yourself. You kissed me back yesterday."

"It was instinctive."

"My point precisely."

She seemed to be growing more and more annoyed with him, and he took some satisfaction in that.

"I mean," she said calmly, "that it was just a sexual response."

He smiled, recognizing that for the lie that it was. "You're talking to the man who's made love to you many times. You *never* have 'just a sexual response.'" He repeated her words with mild scorn. "You're always heart-and-soul into it."

"A lot of good that did me," she muttered quietly, querulously.

"You didn't stay with it long enough," he chided.

She gave him a direct look. "It's hard to stay 'with it'—" she gave his words the same inflection he'd used when repeating hers "—when the object of the exercise is always haring across the globe to get away from you."

Gabrielle belched loudly.

"That's an appropriate response to such a ridiculous accusation." He settled the baby back into his arm and gave her the bottle again. "I wasn't trying to get away from you, and you know it. You just couldn't live with the reality that other people need me, too."

Michelle was no longer sucking, but simply staring with a wide-eyed and slightly worried expression. Harper put the bottle aside and stood to walk across the room with her, patting her back. "I don't think we should argue when we're holding the babies." She reached the window and turned back to fix him with a firm expression. "It'll make them tense."

"Fine," he replied amiably. "I don't want to argue."

A flare of self-satisfaction shone in her eyes. "Good. Then it's agreed—all we talk about is the house and the babies."

Wanting to growl, he remembered instead that reverse psychology had worked last night. Maybe it would work again. If it didn't, he wasn't above ignoring her directive.

"All right, you win. No more talking about us. Just the twins and the furniture."

She was quiet a moment. He couldn't help but wonder if that meant she was simply surprised—or disappointed.

WHILE THE TWINS WERE NAPPING in the afternoon, Dillon went from room to room making notes on a yellow pad. Harper straightened what little needed to be straightened.

Peg had washed and changed the bedding in the downstairs bedroom before she left, and Skye had made a grocery list of things for Darrick and Dillon to purchase on their way home from the bank that morning. The larder was full.

That meant there was nothing left for Harper to do but go up into the attic and move her things to another room. Skye had suggested that she use Duncan's room so that she could be handy if Dillon had trouble with the twins during the night.

She was surprised to find the attic stairs already pulled down and Dillon sitting cross-legged near the dress form, making notes. He had the twins in their carrier beside him, fast asleep.

He looked up from his notes as she stepped off the ladder onto the attic floor.

"Sorry," he said, preparing to stand. "I thought you were in the kitchen."

She stayed him with a raised hand. "You're fine. I was just getting my things to move into Duncan's room. Skye thought I should."

He looked indulgently amused. "And your decision to move had nothing to do with...Ophelia?"

"Olivia," she corrected, "and I'm moving because Skye thought I should be handier to you during the night." She regretted the words even before she'd finished the sentence.

His look turned predatory. "An excellent idea."

"Handier to the babies." She tried to quell his amusement with a withering look. It didn't work.

"Of course," he said, finally letting it go. "But you can't blame me for asking. Every time I suggest something to you, you fight with me. I thought there must be something else behind your decision to cooperate."

"There is," she said, kneeling down before her sleeping bag and beginning to roll it up. "Skye isn't you."

Dillon went back to his notes, shrugging off the jab.

"That's nice for Darrick, isn't it?" she asked, tying the feather down bag into a tight roll. "That he's found somebody. And that she seems wonderful." She reached toward a small stack of clothes that was closer to Dillon than to her.

He transferred his pen to his left hand, then took the stack of clothes in his right and held it toward her. Somewhere in the transfer the stack fell, silk and lace raining to the floor. He was left with the small cup of a black lace bra hooked on one finger.

He held it up, pretending to inspect it. "I see the biceps flexes haven't really helped," he observed.

She snatched it from him, biting back a laugh. Her small chest had always been a joke between them. She'd never been offended because she'd never detected any lack of appreciation in him for her meager proportions.

"No, they haven't," she admitted. "And the glutes squeezes haven't reduced anything, either."

"I noticed," he said with an appreciative glance at her hips as she bent to retrieve the disassembled pile of underwear. "And I'm glad. That's one of your best features."

"Don't start being nice," she said, stuffing the underwear into her sport bag. "You'll confuse me."

"It's interesting the way you do that," he said mildly, continuing to make notes. "Argue with everything I say until I'm at the end of my patience, then blame me when it frays."

"When we disagree—" she picked up her sleeping bag, walked to the ladder, and threw the bag down the hall to the corridor below "—why do you believe I'm arguing with you instead of *you* being the one who's arguing with *me?*"

"Because you're the one who always starts it. You're the one who has to legislate everything."

A hot reply came to the tip of her tongue as she walked back to pick up her bag. But she bit it back, remembering the sleeping babies.

"I thought we weren't going to talk about us."

"See?" He pointed his pen at her. "You just did it again."

She took instant offense but kept her voice down. "You're the one who brought up my flat chest!"

"Well...you dropped a bra in my hand. I couldn't

help myself.'' He laughed as he got to his feet. ''Anything I can carry down for you?''

''No, you have the babies.''

''That's all right. You stay with them and I'll come right back.''

She held up the small bag. ''This is all I have. I only expected to be here the weekend.''

He took it from her. ''I've got it.''

Harper stopped near the dress form, a sudden and curious feeling of...what?—warmth? energy?—wafting around her. It wasn't the cold wind created by the presence of a ghost that one always read about in books. It was warm, embracing. Comforting.

And very, very unsettling.

''Dillon?'' she called, alarmed.

''Yeah?'' He turned at the attic stairs, then dropped the bag and came back to her, his hands reaching out. ''What?'' He looked at the form. ''Olivia?''

Unconsciously, she held on to him. ''I don't know,'' she whispered. ''Did you feel anything?''

''No. You did?''

She nodded. ''A sort of...warmth.''

His expression was carefully neutral. Clearly, he didn't believe her, but didn't want to tell her that she was crazy. She appreciated that, because she was beginning to think so herself.

''Come on.'' He put an arm around her shoulders and drew her toward the stairs. ''Small change of plans. You go down first. I'll toss you the bag, then I'll bring the twins down.''

It was a plan designed so that she wouldn't have to stay upstairs alone. She appreciated that, too.

In a matter of minutes, they had her things in Duncan's room, and were downstairs in the kitchen. He

pushed her into a chair at the table, placed the carrier
with the sleeping babies on the counter, then put the
kettle on.

"I thought I saw a box of tea in here," he said,
moving cans and boxes aside in the cupboard.

"Bottom shelf," she said, rubbing her arms. "Behind the turning rack of spices."

"Ah. Right. Hold on. Almost ready." He pulled
down a pair of mugs. "Tea always made everything
right for you."

Harper watched Dillon work and knew she was in
big trouble. She was fairly certain she'd just had a minor brush with the paranormal—if any such contact
could ever be considered minor. Yet lust moved rest-
lessly in her as her eyes followed Dillon around the
kitchen.

A ghost from her past, messing with her ability to
cope with what seemed to be a ghost in her present.

This was not good.

Not good at all.

Chapter Five

"Do *you* believe in ghosts?" Harper asked Michelle. She lay with the twins on a blanket on the living room floor, while Dillon prepared lunch. The babies lay on their backs; she lay on her stomach, propped between them on her elbows.

Michelle stared at her with wide, intense eyes, little arms flailing the air.

"What about you?" Harper focused on Gabrielle, a clone of her sister. The baby smiled at her.

Harper laughed, amazed by the precious infants. She couldn't believe how different they seemed already from the newborns she'd seen at Darrick's home in Edenfield when they were only several days old.

"Well, I'm asking because I think we've got one," she explained as the babies watched her intently. "I don't think she's one of those mean ones you hear about that breaks things and drags chains around, but she makes me a little nervous all the same. I think she wants to make friends with me and, well, you know, I'd like all my friends to be this side of the great divide, if you know what I mean."

Four little arms flailed and two tiny mouths worked into perfect little Os. "I thought you'd understand."

She smoothed a dark spike of hair on Michelle, who tended to look as though she'd been electrified. "So what do you want to do today? Shall we go check out the mall?"

Gabrielle's little foot kicked Harper in the chin when she leaned too close.

"You're right," Harper said, rubbing her chin as she leaned out of reach. "They probably don't even have one here. But there must be some place where we can shop. I'm not sharing my makeup with you, you know. You'll have to get your own stuff."

Michelle emitted a little whine. Harper put a hand to her stomach and rubbed gently. "I know you'd prefer the natural look, but I want to use you two in an ad campaign. It was all your aunt Skye's idea, and she did it just to pressure me into staying because—I don't know if you know this—but your whole family is trying to get your father and me back together."

Michelle's uncoordinated gyrations caused her little hand to slap against Harper's.

"Well, it wasn't my fault," Harper explained in a high, quiet voice. "I loved him to pieces, but security's very important to me, you know? I'm not talking about money and all that, because I can make my own. But my parents died when I was quite young. My aunts were very loving, but they were all over the place, and I went from one to the other while they carried on their careers and tried to raise me at the same time. I don't want to live like that as an adult, and I don't want my children to. And you know how your father is. Well, maybe you don't yet, because you thought Darrick was your father."

Michelle began to cry in earnest.

"I know you're upset and I don't blame you." Harper, who'd been wearing two pacifiers on an index finger like some eccentric opera ring, pulled one off and teased it into Michelle's mouth. The baby stopped crying. "Your life's been rather confusing so far, hasn't it? But we're trying to get it straightened out for you. The important thing to remember is that you have so many people who love you. We're just not absolutely sure who you belong to yet."

Harper turned to Gabrielle, who smiled at her again. She put a fingertip to the baby's button nose. "Anyway, your dad—Dillon—runs around the world taking care of people who are sick and injured, and while that's very noble, I suspect there's more than nobility behind it. I think he's on the run from something. I know he acts like he can handle anything, but we all have our weaknesses." She sighed as both babies watched her contentedly. "And I guess I have to face the fact that he'll always be one of mine."

It was only then that Harper noticed the shoes. There were two of them, right in front of her face, just beyond the blanket. They were brown Dexters. And there was someone in them.

Dillon.

"One of your what?" he asked as he set a pair of plates on the coffee table in front of the loveseat. He offered her a hand up.

"One of the banes of my existence," she said as she took his hand, horrified at the notion that he might have heard her admit she was sometimes still weak for him.

"I had to ask," he said in self-derision as he pulled the rocker up to the other side of the loveseat. "I've half a mind to reclaim my sandwich."

"Wow." Harper sat amid the ratty cushions, admiring the thick sandwich held closed with a toothpick, professionally beaded with a green olive and a chunk of cucumber. "What is it?"

"Just avocado and veggies." He knelt on the edge of the blanket to turn the babies so that they could watch them. Then he took the chair facing the loveseat. "Want to go shopping this afternoon? Do some reconnoitering for furniture and the other things we need?"

"Sure." Harper loved to haunt specialty shops and secondhand stores, a passion she had in common with Dillon's parents. Except that she liked to think she had more conventional taste. Unfortunately, antique shops had been off-limits to her for the past year.

"What did you do with that dry sink we refinished?" She pulled up a toothpick, then caught the olive in her teeth and slipped it off.

"I still have it."

Michelle fussed, and Dillon leaned sideways out of his chair to replace the pacifier she'd lost. "You have to hold on to what you want, baby," he said, smiling at her. She responded with wild kicks. He rubbed Gabrielle's foot, and she smiled at him around her pacifier. "I have plants in the top," he said, straightening and picking up his sandwich. "And dishes Mom and Dad gave me stored in the bottom."

Harper remembered the day they'd bought the sink at a flea market in Astoria. Dillon had just returned from a week in Hong Kong helping victims of a collapsed hotel. She'd been pouting because she was happy to see him and didn't want to bring up his absences and how they were beginning to upset her, but was still annoyed that he didn't see how much she needed him, too.

He'd driven her to the little town at the mouth of the Columbia River, knowing how much she liked it there. She'd finally relaxed and they'd had a wonderful day.

But he'd been gone again before they'd even refinished the sink. She stayed to complete the project, sent his clothes to the Northwest Medical Team as a sort of safety-valve release of emotion, then taken an apartment.

He'd returned a week later, they'd had a terrible quarrel on her doorstep, then she'd slammed the door in his face. That was when he'd nailed her door closed.

Now Dillon looked around the living room. "Might look good somewhere in here. Or did you want it— since you finished it?"

She shook her head, chewing the cucumber, then she swallowed. "You bought it."

"For you."

"I...don't need it." She took a sip from one of the tall glasses of iced tea he'd also placed on the table. "My place isn't that big." She pointed through to the dining room. "It'd look nice on the wall that abuts the kitchen. Or maybe in the kitchen where that pew is."

"I like the pew."

"I do, too. But maybe it could go in the upstairs hall."

He nodded thoughtfully. "Good idea."

"There's a shop you'll like downtown, near the old hotel," she said. "Dori and I wandered through on a walk. Their stock is a step up from secondhand, but not antiquey enough to be really expensive. And I'll have a day or two to help you refinish whatever you buy."

He nodded. "All right. We'll check it out. I suppose your place is filled with all kinds of great stuff you freshened up for a song?"

"I wish." She smiled ruefully. "Actually, it's filled with a very pedestrian matching sofa and chair from Furniture & Fixtures—and other stuff. I have no dining room, just a little bar in the kitchen, and my bed is just a frame. I do have a huge walk-in closet with more space than I'll ever need, so I haven't even looked for a dresser yet. Wade and I've made a monster with the business."

Dillon angled one leg over the other and made a disparaging sound. "I'm sure Wade makes a monster out of whatever he touches. I'm surprised *you* haven't sprouted horns and fangs yet."

Harper's amiable mood disintegrated abruptly. "I'm glad you said that. It proves how wrong you were about *me* always being the one who takes issue with everything *you* say. I was trying to tell you about myself, and you had to be rude. Thank you. And just to set the record straight, Wade *doesn't* touch me."

His expression was clearly skeptical. "Like I'd believe that. You always look guilty when you talk about Seattle."

Despite her best efforts, the surprise remark caught her off guard and she went crimson. "What do you mean?" She forced indignation into her voice, but it was too breathy from fear to be effective.

He narrowed his gaze on her analytically. "You're doing it right now. You've got a little something going on in Seattle, haven't you?"

Ignoring the second half of her sandwich, she picked up her plate, knowing that she had to leave or that she would be sorry. "Well, if you're not going to believe what I tell you, there's no point in talking to you, is there?" And she left the room.

She stomped back a moment later to retrieve her iced tea, then disappeared again.

Dillon turned to the twins, who were still watching him contentedly. He leaned down and said quietly, "When you grow up and have arguments with the men in your life, don't walk out on them, okay? It's very annoying. And don't be this touchy. If you're going to leave a great guy to take up with a jerk, you have to expect a little needling, am I right?"

DILLON SECURED THE NOW sleeping babies in their car seats in the back seat of the crew cab of his truck. Then he stood by the open door on the driver's side, his arm hooked in the lowered window, certain Harper would appear at any moment.

No matter how annoyed she was with him, she wouldn't pass up an opportunity to go furniture shopping. She loved nothing better than to dress in grubbies and kneel on newspaper surrounded by stripping agents and paint, facing a chair or a table that looked beyond repair or redemption.

Some of his fondest memories of her were with her hair disheveled, her face smudged, and her eyes glowing with the excitement of the project. That and her tendency to sing show tunes while she worked. He'd learned the entire score of *Phantom of the Opera* while she stripped and repainted an old picket fence that ran completely around his half-acre property.

He heard a sound from the second story and looked up to see Harper leaning from Duncan's bedroom window.

"Are you coming?" he called.

She placed her hands on the sill. "Where are you going?"

"To find that shop you were talking about."

She put a hand to her heart in theatrical surprise. "You mean you *believed* me about the shop?"

He might have had that coming, but he ignored it. "There's a frappuccino in it for you," he bribed.

She studied him a little stiffly for a moment, the sunlight turning her hair to platinum. "I'll be right down," she said finally.

She ran out the front door a moment later in jeans and a white shirt, a colorful hank of fabric crushed in one hand, a big straw purse slung over her shoulder.

"What's that?" he asked as he held the passenger door open for her. "Something that requires shoes to match that's going to prevent us from serious furniture shopping?"

"Nooo." She drew the word out exasperatedly as she held up the cloth front packs Bertie had made for carrying the babies. "I thought these'd leave your hands free for doing all the inspecting you like to annoy shop owners with when you're buying something. Geez." She studied the long distance from the ground to the floor of the truck. "This thing should come with a fiberglass pole."

"No pole," he said, scooping her off the ground. She uttered a little cry of surprise. "But it does come with the McKeon Reunion free-throw champion." He dropped her on the seat with a little bounce.

"Lucky for me," she said a little breathlessly.

He grinned. "I've been telling you that for years." He closed the door, climbed in behind the wheel and headed for town.

THE AFTERNOON WAS SUNNY and warm. Miraculously, both babies had allowed the transfer from car seat to front pack without waking.

Standing in the parking lot, Harper pointed to the letters painted on the awning over the rear entrance of the hotel. "The Buckley Arms," she read, as Dillon started toward the shop next door. "I wonder if it's the same Buckleys."

Dillon stopped to wait for her. "Considering the size of the town, it's pretty likely."

She stared up at the hotel, eyes shaded against the sun. "Maybe someone there would know about Olivia."

"I thought you were afraid of Olivia."

"Well…Skye wants to know."

He opened his mouth to dispute that, then changed his mind. It was too nice a day. And a friendly if fragile rapport had been reestablished.

He took the few steps back to her, caught her hand, and pulled her after him to the rear entrance of Used But Enthused.

The place was a gold mine, Dillon decided after a careful look around. It contained used furniture of all kinds and for every room, light fixtures, trunks, dolls, dishware, and a few pieces of old clothing.

"All right," he said to Harper under his breath as they inspected a chest of drawers and a pair of matching bedside tables some misguided soul had painted magenta. "You deserve high praise for finding this place."

"Keep the praise," she returned softly. "I'll take my pay in gold and chocolate, thank you."

"I did promise you a frappuccino."

"That'll do. Where are you thinking of putting this dresser?"

"My room," he said. "I like the simple lines." He scratched a chip of paint off with his fingernail on the inside of a drawer. "Oak. Thought so. See anything you like?"

She pointed against a far wall. "There's a steamer trunk in poor repair that's a real steal. I can reline and refinish it so it'll look great at the foot of your bed."

She looked so interested, so eager, that he felt a catch in his chest. He'd forgotten how much fun it used to be to have her on his side.

"I used to like *you* at the foot of my bed," he said, "stretched out and watching TV while I did paperwork."

That surprised her, and for a moment he saw a look in her eyes that defined precisely what he felt. Then it was gone, and she said seriously, "You have to stop doing that."

"No, I don't."

She met his eyes, but before he could read the expression in hers, the clerk approached, asking if he could help.

It was an hour and a half before the back of Dillon's truck was loaded with their finds. The babies were still asleep, so he took her to a little coffee bar in the hotel for the promised frappuccino.

The hotel was classically Victorian with dark wood and potted palms everywhere and a thickly upholstered circular bench ranged around a central column in the lobby.

The coffee bar was off to the right in a little alcove. Harper immediately engaged the young man behind the bar in conversation. The hotel was named after the founding Buckleys, the young man told her in answer to her questions, but they were all long gone from Dancer's Beach.

"Right," Harper said, "but I was wondering if you knew anything about them. The older brother, particularly."

"There's some stuff at the library..."

"Yes. I've seen that."

"And some things in the museum at Lincoln City."

"But nothing in this hotel?"

The young man began to shake his head, then stopped, reconsidering. "Actually, there *was* an envelope of stuff my mom found in the attic."

"Your mom?"

The young man smiled proudly. "My parents own the place. I'll see if she can come out." He reached for the phone on the wall and spoke to his mother while concocting their drinks. "Right," he said. "They're customers, and the lady's interested in the Buckleys." He listened a moment. "Yeah, she knows about all that stuff. She'd like to see the things you found in the attic. Okay." He replaced the receiver and handed their drinks across the counter. "She'll be right out." He pointed them to a small round table surrounded by pub chairs.

Dillon pulled Harper's chair out, leaving sufficient room for the baby tied to the front of her. "I can't believe Michelle's cooperating like this," he said, gently patting the back of the baby attached to him.

"I know." Harper sipped her drink and closed her eyes in approval. "That is *so* good. I think Michelle wakes up so often because she doesn't want to miss anything. Some baby radar lets her know when something's going on that we're hoping she'll sleep through."

She seemed to hesitate a moment, and Dillon noticed something subtle change in her manner. He didn't know what it was, but he felt it as though he had his own radar. He thought ruefully that he probably did—where she was concerned.

"I suppose," she added, "she must come by that naturally if her mother's a world news reporter."

Allison. It was the first time she'd been mentioned between them since the conversation in which he'd learned Harper couldn't be the twins' mother. Dillon wondered how much it had cost Harper to bring Allison up so casually. He was silent for a moment, choosing his words carefully.

"It's true that she never missed anything," he confirmed. "And she did have a knack for annoying anyone who tried to keep information from her."

"She always looks so fearless on television." Harper stirred the contents of her glass with the straw. Then she glanced up at Dillon, her eyes filled with a kind of jealousy that seemed to be without hostility. "I imagine men find that a very seductive quality in a woman."

He wasn't sure if he agreed with that or not. "I suppose it's admirable," he conceded finally, "but I'm not sure I found it seductive."

She looked at him steadily. "You obviously found *something* seductive."

He thought back to the night he and Allison had spent together, and shook his head. "As I recall, it was her vulnerability that finally brought us together. She'd been holding a baby while I worked on the baby's mother, then the baby died right there in Allie's arms. She cried in *my* arms all the way to London that night when another crew relieved my team and she got called back home." He sighed heavily, his eyes still focused on the memory. "We made love to strengthen each other. Our jobs require us to remain somewhat removed so that we can function, but your heart doesn't know that and it goes through a wringer when babies start dying around you." He rubbed the little round bundle in his front pack.

"I'm sorry." She wanted to stop that look in his eyes. She knew what a good doctor he was and how much he cared. She could only imagine what the horrors he described could do to him. "I didn't intend to pry, or dredge up difficult memories, I was just... wondering."

He came back to her then, and to their intimate little table. "Wondering?" He mulled over her carefully chosen word. "A little jealous, maybe?"

"Yeah," she said, her tone implying just the opposite. "Right."

He challenged her with a look she ignored as a middle-aged woman in a blue skirt and sweater approached their table.

"Fran Boswell." She introduced herself to Dillon as he stood to pull out a chair for her. Then, noticing first one baby, then the other, she added, "Well, my goodness. Twins? I suppose people who have them get used to them, but to the rest of us, it always seems so remarkable. They're identical?"

Dillon nodded. "This is Michelle." He patted the baby he held, then pointed to the baby dozing against Harper's breast. "And that's Gabrielle. I'm Dillon McKeon, and this is Harper Harriman." After admiring the babies, Fran shook his hand, then thanked him as he seated her.

"My brothers and I have bought—" he began.

"The old Buckley house," Fran Boswell finished for

him. "Yes, I know. Everyone knows. No wonder you're interested in the family."

Harper's eyes went to the faded manila envelope that the woman held in her hand. "Jeremy says you've seen what the library has, and that you've been to the museum."

"We haven't been to the museum," Harper corrected, tearing her eyes from the envelope to smile politely at the woman. "But Dillon's brother's wife, who is really the one interested in all of this—" she ignored Dillon's raised eyebrow, clearly questioning her denial of responsibility for the investigation "—has talked to Bertie Fisher about it, and Bertie knows Millie Dawson, the great-granddaughter of Joshua and Sarajane Buckley. Joshua was the second brother. Millie says the museum doesn't have the information we're looking for."

Fran nodded. "And what is that?"

"I'm looking for details about Olivia Marbury."

"Ah." Fran nodded again. "The dancer Barton Buckley *didn't* marry."

"Yes. But Olivia went to the Klondike when he married India Winfield, and he went, too, after India died."

Fran raised an eyebrow. "Did he? I didn't know that."

"Dillon's sister-in-law found it in another book about regional history. It's just a mention that he signed on to a ship that left Portland for Alaska. Our suspicion is that he went searching for Olivia."

"Are you writing a book?"

"No. I'm just…interested. We've found something we think might have belonged to her."

"Oh. Well, I don't think I have anything that could clear up any of that for you." Fran pinched the clasp on the envelope and opened it. "All I have really are a few things that had fallen behind a drawer in an old desk that had been stored upstairs. When my husband and I bought the place, I thought it would be fun to have the desk in my office, but it isn't big enough. I think it must have been Alice's desk. She and Matthew owned the hotel, you know. The rolltop's beautiful, of course, but there isn't enough surface space to work comfortably."

Harper made a mental note to ask Fran if she could see the desk, but wished she would stop talking about it and open the envelope.

Fran did just that. The contents were pretty spare: an old receipt for linens, a narrow length of pink silk ribbon, a hairpin, a recipe and two photos.

"May I?" Harper asked, indicating the photos.

Fran placed them in her hands. "I should have given them to the museum, I suppose, but I really don't want to part with them. I've kind of grown attached to them."

In the first photo, a man and a woman looked back at Harper, the man tall and dark with a natty mustache, the woman small and slender and looking just a little stunned. Harper couldn't decipher whether that expression meant she was happy with whatever had surprised her, or saddened by it.

Her heart began to beat a little faster.

She'd looked through the books she'd promised to return to the library for Skye, and she knew from them that the man was Barton. But was the woman India or Olivia? India had been described as robust, but then corsets in those days could make any woman appear petite.

The man wore an evening suit complete with top hat.

The woman was clearly dressed for a ball or the opera in a slim-waisted gown with ballooning sleeves caught just above her elbows and trimmed with lace. Large ribbons were tied where the sleeves connected with the bodice, and long streamers trailed from them almost to the hem of the dress. There were two plumes in her pale hair, and she carried a fan.

"I thought of her as a brunette." Harper was unaware she'd spoken the words aloud until Dillon's hand gently clasped her arm, as though to force her back to the present.

"That could be India," he said. "Or someone else entirely. Don't jump to conclusions."

Harper smiled at him. "Of course not." Then she asked Fran, "Who are these people?" She held up the second photo of a different man and woman, the woman holding a baby whose long christening gown flowed over her arm.

Fran shrugged. "I couldn't tell you."

"I don't suppose you'd want to risk exposing this to the light of a copier?"

Fran considered her a moment, then took the photo back. Harper's heart sank a little.

Then Fran returned everything to the envelope and handed it to Harper. "Tell you what. You can borrow it for a little while, but I do want it back. I'd like to know who's in the picture, too."

Harper was delighted. "Thank you!" she said. "I promise to take good care of everything in the envelope. And I'll have it back to you as quickly as I can."

"Good. Well." Fran pushed away from the table and stood. "I've got to get back to work. It was nice meeting both of you. You've made such beautiful babies."

Harper hadn't realized until that moment that Fran

had assumed they were husband and wife. Of course, that was the logical assumption. She found it curiously painful to correct her. "Actually, Dillon and I are just friends. I'm helping him furnish the house, and I thought I'd be a sport and carry one of the babies."

Fran pushed her chair in. "So, your wife's at home?" she asked Dillon.

Dillon cast Harper a glance that suggested things would have been easier all around if she hadn't felt compelled to explain. "No, I'm not married," he said.

"Oh." Harper could see the confusion cloaked by good manners in the woman's face. "Well. Good luck. Looks like a big job to tackle alone." She took several steps back from the table and waved at Harper. "I'll wait to hear from you."

As though to make up for their exemplary behavior all day, both babies screamed all the way home. Neither bottles nor pacifiers would placate them.

"Maybe they just need to stretch their little muscles after so much time in the packs," Dillon said, putting them on a blanket on the loveseat and trying in vain to charm them out of their tantrums.

Meanwhile Harper warmed bottles. She returned at a run, quieting each little mouth with the magical nipple.

Dillon picked up Gabrielle; Harper scooped up Michelle; and they settled on the loveseat unconsciously leaning against each other.

"That was a successful shopping trip." Harper basked in the glow of the moment, and the memory of the pleasant afternoon. "Reminded me of the old days when we prowled every little shop in the valley for a project to work on."

He smiled, apparently enjoying that memory, too.

"Of course we didn't have babies stuck to us like mistletoe on oak trees."

Harper wasn't sure if it was the mention of mistletoe or indulging the memory of happy times together that opened a floodgate of sensory impressions from their shared past. She could remember very specifically, visually and in color, lying under him in the middle of his large bed on the very brink of fulfilment, and seeing love in his eyes as he smoothed the hair from her face.

She could also recall, as though she were reliving it, the touch of his thumb against her temple, his breath on her cheek, the thrust of his manhood deeper inside her as the sound of her little gasps punctured the quiet.

Then she felt the power of their mutual climax, the shudders of superlative pleasure that evolved slowly into a delicious contentment.

In the moment that it took her to realize that she was experiencing memory and not the here and now, reality drilled a hole beneath her feet and she fell in. Darkness consumed her.

"What?" Dillon asked anxiously.

She guessed by the look on his face that her sudden sense of loss was visible.

"Ah..." She searched for a credible excuse. "I'd forgotten how exhausting shopping is."

He continued to study her, obviously suspecting her excuse. "Don't you do it anymore?"

She shook her head, forcing a smile. "I told you. Just no...no place to put anything."

She didn't think he believed her, but he seemed willing to accept her fib.

"Well, I hate to bring this up if you're tired," he said, "but we still have to empty the truck. Looks like rain tonight."

She fought to struggle out of the net of memories and to reestablish their adversarial relationship—which was so much safer. "*You* have to empty the truck," she said. "Somebody has to stay with the girls."

He grinned. "So you're going to pull this on me now every time there's some chore you don't like doing?"

"Darn right. I'm a volunteer, remember? The hard stuff's your job."

"We used to have a fifty-fifty thing going for us."

She cast him a wry glance. "I'm a stand-in nanny, not a significant other. Now we have a five-ninety-five thing going."

"Whoa. Do you think Olivia would approve of that attitude?"

"I thought you didn't believe in Olivia."

He hitched a shoulder. Gabrielle's little head rose and fell with the movement but she didn't miss a beat on the bottle. "I don't," he said quietly. "But I believe in you. So I can't just dismiss what's on your mind."

That was unsettling. "I appreciate that," she admitted grudgingly. "But Olivia went to the Klondike. I don't think we're dealing with a shrinking violet here."

"Just my point," he countered. "She gave herself one hundred percent to everything."

"If you remember," she said, wondering how it was that no matter what they discussed, she always found herself up against the barrier of their relationship, "she couldn't give that to Barton because he refused it."

Her implication was clear.

And so was Dillon's sudden exasperation. "I'd tell you I never refused anything you tried to give me, but there seems to be little point. You're determined to be the tragic figure that Olivia was."

"I don't think she was tragic," she disputed, her

throat thick with emotion. "She bravely struck out on her own, and that's what I did."

"Then why is it so important to you," he asked, "to believe that Barton found her?"

He was right. Perhaps some illogical cranny in her brain had decided that proof of Olivia's ultimate happiness would somehow make up for the loss of her own.

"Love legends should have happy endings," she said, glancing down at the baby whose eyes were beginning to close. "But we know better than to expect that from real life."

It was the point in the conversation when she would have walked away—had she not been holding a baby who was on the brink of sleep. She simply gave Dillon a look that told him the subject was closed.

"We'll discuss this again," he said, "when we don't have babies in our arms."

"It's hopeless."

He shook his head at her. "*You're* hopeless. The argument is not. It *will* be continued."

Chapter Six

While Michelle and Gabrielle slept, worn out by their enthusiastic eating, Harper did help Dillon haul their purchases inside. He managed most of the heavier pieces himself, with just a little help easing them from the back of the truck to the dolly he'd bought at a hardware store on the way home.

Harper carried in the nightstands, an old lamp in terrible repair whose dragon-shaped stand had intrigued both of them, and the trunk. The big pieces went into the garage where they would be refinished, but Harper carried the trunk into Duncan's room where she would be sleeping.

It was a simple, flat-topped trunk rather than the camel-back trunk prized by collectors, but it was sturdy—if a little unsightly at the moment. She'd spotted a handful of herbs in a corner of it when she'd inspected it at the shop and that had made her want it all the more.

She reached into the trunk now and scooped up the little quarter-size cluster of lavender and rose petals, and she spied, nestled in their midst, one single dark-blue sequin. She smiled at the thought that early in the century, a woman with a glittery dark blue dress had folded her treasures into this trunk.

"I thought that was mine," Dillon teased from the doorway of Duncan's room. He leaned a shoulder against the molding, his arms folded.

Harper looked up guiltily, her hand closed around the little pinch of herbs. "If I keep it in here, I can work on it for you at night."

He took several steps into the room. "Won't you be sleeping at night?"

"Sometimes I can't."

"Since when?" He came to lean over her and inspect the torn and stained beige-and-brown patterned lining, and the shallow little drawer that nested in the top.

She opened her hand to show him the herbs. "Look what I found."

His long, slender index finger isolated the sequin. "What have we here? Something from a showgirl costume, maybe?"

She chuckled. "That's fun to think about. It's probably just from an evening dress. Sequins were big in the teens and twenties."

He squatted down beside her to look into her eyes, apparently not at all distracted by her find. "How long have you not been sleeping?"

"I sleep," she said defensively, dropping the herbs back into the drawer. Then she dusted off her hands. "Just not very long sometimes."

"Why not?"

"Because I'm in business for myself," she said, closing the lid on the trunk. *Because I'm often up half the night,* she added silently to herself, *and I'm not going to tell you why.* "And I'm doing well, so that means I have a lot of things on my mind. It just…goes with the territory.''

The steady sleeplessness had started after his parents' anniversary party, when she'd thought for a glorious few hours that she and Dillon were back together again. The sense of loss had been greater after the second breakup. And the loneliness seemed to run deeper. During the day, she could put it away by keeping busy, but at night…

His eyes went over her face, as though looking for signs of weariness. She pushed at her hair self-consciously.

"You always slept like a rock when we were together," he said. "In fact, you're the only person I know who can be in full conversation one instant, and fast asleep the next.''

With a casual toss of her head, she pushed to her feet. "I was young and innocent then.''

He stood also. "That was only two years ago.''

"Well…change can happen quickly.''

"Can't you just admit that you miss me?''

Because she couldn't help herself, she conceded quietly, "I miss you. There. But how does that help?'' Then she pushed the trunk against the wall. "For two people who decided *not* to talk about their relationship, we certainly end up there a lot.''

He remained in the middle of the room, apparently as surprised by her admission as she was. He watched her as she fiddled with the trunk's torn leather straps. "I like knowing that.'' His rich, deep voice bridged the space between them, reaching her like the stroke of a hand. "You look as though there's more you'd like to tell me.''

She flushed guiltily again and turned away. She wished he'd stop reading her mind.

He came up behind her, his hands falling gently on her shoulders. "Can you admit that you still love me?"

"No." She pulled herself together and moved beyond his reach. "We're over. You've had babies with another woman and I—I'm too busy to think about anything but my business."

The silence was thick for one long moment. "Then what is it you're not telling me?" he asked finally.

A loud wail came from Dillon's room. He looked first frustrated, then resigned as he backed toward the door. "Michelle," he said. "Obviously sensing a significant argument she doesn't want to miss."

Thunder rolled in the distance as Harper followed to help, thanking heaven—and Michelle—for the reprieve.

"At the rate we argue," she muttered, "that baby's insomnia's going to be far worse than mine."

DILLON HEARD MOVEMENT in the room across the hall. A glance at the illuminated dial of his watch told him that it was 2:45 a.m. The twins were fast asleep, but it sounded as though Harper was awake. And so was he.

He'd been a little premature in congratulating himself on getting her to stay for a few days, he realized. She was helpful and polite, and when she let her guard down revealed glimpses of the old Harper he'd fallen in love with the moment she'd backed her car into his in the parking lot of his clinic.

But she was determined to keep him at a safe distance, and, if his instincts were correct, to keep something from him. He'd caught that guilty look in her eyes several times now.

He'd begun to wonder if she'd lied about mothering the twins, but he'd seen that photo of her taken the month before they were born. She had clearly not been pregnant.

So what was it? She was making a precarious situation even more difficult.

Difficult, he thought resolutely, but not impossible. He prided himself on finding solutions to problems when everyone else had given up.

Of course, the parameters of the problem she posed were cosmic in scope. He would not have imagined when he'd completed his residency at Oregon Health Sciences University and opened his own clinic, determined to save the world, that he'd have been stopped dead in his tracks by a woman weighing one hundred and three pounds.

Well, okay, he wasn't dead, but he was definitely wounded. He just didn't enjoy his life without her.

He started to crawl out of his sleeping bag, but thought the better of it. If he went to check on her, one of two things would happen. Either they'd argue again, or she'd be in one of her mellow moods and she'd give him that wistful look that told him she was unhappy, too. But if he tried to do anything about it she'd remind him that the mother of his twins was out there, somewhere, and that what he and Harper had once shared was over.

But it wasn't. It would never be.

Invincible problem-solver that he was, he'd better come up with a solution—and fast.

"YOU SURE YOU'LL BE OKAY alone with them for a couple of hours?" Dillon asked, hoping for reassurance. It was just after lunch on Wednesday, and he was going to town to buy beds. Michelle had been particularly fussy all day, and the prospect of shopping with her wasn't appealing.

"We'll be fine." Harper walked him to the door, Michelle whining in the front pack she wore. Gabrielle was asleep in her carrier on the settee.

"Anything we need while I'm out?" he asked from the porch, beyond which rain was falling heavily.

"Chocolate," she said.

"Aren't we low on tea?"

"Yes, but I'm leaving tomorrow."

He ignored that and ran to the truck, dodging rain.

When Michelle finally dozed off an hour later, Harper brought the babies upstairs and placed their carrier on her sleeping bag. Then she called her aunt Cleo. There was no answer.

She fought a little bout of loneliness, then thought about calling Aunt Phyl. But Phyl and Aggie were still on the cruise.

Now frustrated as well as lonely, Harper knelt to admire her work on the trunk. She'd cleaned the tin and had polished the wooden bands and the brass screws and clasps so that outside, at least, the trunk was a thing of beauty.

She spent the precious quiet time adhering a silver-gray padded fabric to the inside of the trunk. While she worked, she imagined Dillon folding away clothes in it—and to her chagrin, her mind somehow formed the clothes he held into a tuxedo, a cummerbund, collars and cuffs. Wedding clothes!

She dismissed the thought quickly. Or tried to. But despite herself, her fertile imagination even populated a reception line—everyone in Dillon's family; faces she recognized from the CDN lineup on her television screen; then Dillon, looking gorgeous in the tux, with his arm around Allison Cartier whose flowing red hair was covered by a white picture hat that looked very chic with her slim white silk suit.

On the bride's left, a handsome older couple held the twins.

Being a photographer was sometimes a curse, Harper thought as she turned full attention back to her task. You saw everything—even things that were only potentially there.

Well, she had to stop it. She'd never been one to whine over what didn't work, and she wasn't about to start now. Life was too short.

Trite, she told herself, but philosophical and mature.

She had the bottom and the drawer finished, and the piece cut for the top by the time she heard Dillon's key in the lock.

Then she heard other male voices, banging, the crackle of plastic, then footsteps on the stairs. Before she could get to her feet, two men in coveralls carried an elaborate carved oak headboard into Duncan's room; Dillon followed with the footboard and pieces of the frame.

"Wow." Harper moved closer as the men propped the headboard against the walls, took the rails from Dillon and began to assemble the frame.

Dillon smiled at Harper as he picked up the baby carrier. "You like it?"

"It's beautiful," she said.

"You'll get to occupy it tonight. Come on." He gestured for her to follow him. "You and the girls better hide out in Mom and Dad's room until the guys are finished."

"I'll get to sleep in an actual bed?" She ran lightly

down the stairs after him. "You promise? Sleeping bags are fun for a few days, but I've been longing for a featherbed since about Monday."

He stopped at the bottom of the stairs and handed her the carrier. "Yeah, me, too. Just sack out for a little while." He glanced at his watch. "We're having a pizza delivered in about an hour. I took the chance that sausage, onion and green pepper is still your favorite."

It was. She couldn't help smiling at the fact that he remembered that.

"Good," he said. "When the guys are gone, you can help me make up your bed and mine." He rested his hands loosely on his hips and grinned. "Or we could save trouble and just make up one."

She bit back an answering grin and punched his arm. "I told you—you have to stop doing that." She missed his irrepressible sense of humor, even if she didn't miss his cussed tenacity.

"Stop going to bed?" he asked innocently.

"Stop trying to get me to join you," she corrected.

His forehead furrowed. "I remember it being a lot easier in the old days."

"That's because things were a lot simpler in the old days." She turned away from him before she remembered too much, and before his teasing offer could become even more appealing than it already was.

HARPER JOLTED AWAKE to find long shadows in the room and to hear the distant sound of a baby crying. She sat up in bed. "Darian?" she called into the darkness.

Then she remembered where she was and that Darian wasn't here with her—at least not physically.

The twins! She'd only meant to relax for a few

minutes while the men moved the bed. She put a hand down beside her, feeling for the carrier. It was gone.

She scrambled out of bed and followed the sound, unsure whether or not to be alarmed. Running into the kitchen, she found Dillon wearing Gabrielle in one of the packs while holding Michelle in one arm. With his free hand he was warming a bottle in the microwave.

Harper had to give him credit for resourcefulness.

She hurried to help him, taking Michelle and rocking her while she waited for the bottle.

"Sorry I conked out on you," Harper said above the baby's cries.

"No problem," he replied. "I heard you moving around about two this morning. You're probably overdue for a nap."

"I slept through? Did I miss pizza?"

"Yep. I ate it all myself." The microwave ticked for ten seconds, then dinged. Dillon handed her the bottle, his expression grave. "I saved you the box, though, in case you wanted to sniff it and imagine..."

The front doorbell rang and a youthful, cheerful voice shouted through the screen door, "Pizza delivery!"

Harper made a face at Dillon. "You are *so* not funny."

He laughed softly and went to answer.

They sat on the living room floor and watched the news while they ate, the babies lying between them on a blanket.

Later Dillon leaned his back against the settee and sat with the twins on his stomach propped against his knees, while Harper cleaned up.

The muffled sound of a phone ringing caught Harper's attention as she folded a blanket.

Dillon pointed to the jacket on the settee. "Can you get that?" he asked. "It's in my jacket pocket."

She pulled out car keys and a pacifier, then her fingers closed over the cell phone.

"Hello," she said.

"Harper? It's Darrick."

She responded immediately to the worried sound of his voice. "What's the matter?" she demanded, sitting down.

Dillon turned with a questioning frown.

"I hate to tell you this," Darrick said, "but Dori's got the flu. Big-time. She was feeling punk this morning, went to her meeting, then came home sick as a dog."

"I'm sorry." Harper meant that sincerely, and on more than one level. *No, God. No! Yes, God. Thank you, God.* "Here, I'll let you talk to Dillon."

She handed Dillon the phone. "Dori's got the flu," she whispered, then returned to the kitchen, thinking grimly that she knew what this news meant: Dillon was going to ask her to stay.

And in all good conscience, she couldn't leave him alone to deal with two babies by himself. But in the interest of her own mental health, she didn't see how she could stay.

It was becoming more torturous by the hour to be near him and to hold her real feelings in check. If it weren't for the unknown woman who'd given birth to the twins, she'd sit him down right now and tell him how it was.

But she couldn't, and she wouldn't. So she didn't see how she could stay.

Harper made another pot of coffee while Dillon and Darrick talked. She also investigated a white box on the counter, discovering that Dillon had followed through on his promise to come home with chocolate. She popped a peanut cluster in her mouth while she scrubbed the countertops—just for something to do.

She poured fresh coffee and carried the chocolates into the living room, just as Dillon tossed the phone back onto the settee.

"Look," he said, pointing to the television screen. "This is one of Duncan's first films."

Harper turned to the TV to see the colorful titles of an older film. It was entitled *Heart of the Wind*. She'd seen it before. It was the story of a group of friends digging for gold in California; as usual, Duncan was the bad guy.

"What else did Darrick say?" she asked, sitting on the floor beside him. She put the coffee within his reach, but out of the way of the babies, and offered him the box of chocolates.

He shook his head, his eyes on the screen. "No, thanks. They're all yours. Valley Memorial's got a new plastic surgeon. And Skye's decided to get out of the freight business for a while and settle in at home."

Harper turned to stare at him.

"Look! There he is!" He pointed to the screen where Duncan was walking down a dusty California street in typical western gear, a bright bandanna tied around his throat.

"I mean, what did Darrick say about Dori?" she clarified, surprised that she had to.

"Well, she's feeling pretty rotten, I guess. Nothing really major—just gastroenteritis. I imagine it'll be the end of next week before she's up and around."

She braced herself. Now he would ask her to stay. She waited.

He didn't.

She felt abysmally disappointed. He really didn't need her. He was doing fine with the twins by himself. Why would he need a woman who argued with him at every turn?

So, she would just go home tomorrow and that would be that. Over at last. At long last. It was a good thing. Really.

DILLON COULD FEEL HARPER'S confusion, and he understood it perfectly. She'd expected him to plead with her to stay when he heard Dori wouldn't be back for another week. But he wasn't going to. If she wouldn't let him get any closer than an arm's length away, emotionally as well as physically, and if she was going to keep her secrets, whatever they were, then there was little point in her being here anyway.

Except as a stand-in nanny. And she had her own business to run. He couldn't expect her to stay just to help him out.

Besides, reverse psychology had worked so well with her. Maybe he'd get lucky again.

With a slightly hurt expression, she insisted that he stay and finish the film while she put the babies to bed upstairs, one at a time. Then she handed him a mug of coffee with brandy in it and stiffly excused herself to go up, too.

He smiled to himself as her footsteps receded.

HARPER'S ROOM—or rather, Duncan's—was dark and cool. She flipped on the light, and her eyes fell on the new bed. It had been made up and was covered with a rich, jewel-colored quilt. She left the door open so she could hear the babies just across the hall.

With apologies to Duncan for using it before he could, she perched on the end of the bed and bounced lightly up and down.

And that was when she noticed the desk that had been placed near the window. It was a rather small desk as rolltops went, but it had the golden patina of genuine age.

She gasped and stood, walking slowly toward it. The top was raised and many little drawers and cubbyholes were visible. The writing surface was scratched and pitted in a few places, but Harper thought it was the most beautiful thing she'd ever seen.

And she knew what it was. Alice Buckley's desk. The one that Fran Boswell had told them about. Dillon had gone back and bought it.

Harper placed her hands on the desk. The cool wood pressed against her palms and she thought how lucky Duncan was to have such a treasure in his room.

She noticed a white envelope in one of the cubbyholes, then spotted the letters H-A on the protruding end of it.

H-A? She reached tentatively for it and pulled it out a little more. H-A-R-P. No. That wasn't possible.

She pulled it the rest of the way out. H-A-R-P-E-R. Her heart thudding, she opened the envelope and removed a notecard with a little seaside cottage on the front. In Dillon's bold block letters, the message read,

Thank you for putting our differences aside to help me with Michelle and Gabrielle. No matter how small your home is, I'm sure you'll be able to find a place for this. Always yours, Dillon.

Harper could not have been more shocked if a saucer-shaped object had appeared overhead and drawn her up in a beam of light. She pulled aside the small desk chair and sat down. There was air in her lungs, but it wasn't moving. She didn't seem able to draw it in, or to expel it. It just sat there, seeming to expand her midsection, making her heart feel strained and swollen.

What a sweet thing for Dillon to have done. It compensated somewhat for the fact that he hadn't asked her to stay until Dori came back.

She reminded herself that this still didn't mean he needed her; it just said that he appreciated her. She didn't think there was a woman alive who wouldn't react to either expression from a man. Hoping for both was probably pie in the sky.

She was standing in the doorway of her room when he came upstairs ten minutes later.

"Thank you," she said, putting her fidgeting hands in the pockets of her jeans. "I love it."

He smiled affectionately. "I knew you would. I'll have it shipped home for you."

Shipped home. He was expecting her to leave in the morning. Yet his note had closed with "Always yours." Had she grown really dense, she wondered, or was this relationship just too complex and encumbered to allow for understanding?

She decided to bite the bullet. "Would you like me to stay?" she asked, trying very hard to sound as though it didn't matter to her one way or the other.

He'd been about to walk into his room and now turned back. She couldn't read a thing from his expression.

"Would you like to?" he asked.

This was like playing chess with a computer, she thought.

"If you need me," she replied carefully.

He took a step toward her, a shift of expression in his eyes that allowed her to catch a glimpse of something turbulent.

"If I need you for the babies?" he asked, just a touch of aggression in his tone. "Or for me?"

She opened her mouth to reply, but couldn't find an answer.

He evidently got tired of waiting. "Because if all we're going to do for another week is orbit each other, snapping and sparring and never connecting, then I think it'd be better all around if you went back to Wade."

She didn't know what to feel. She wanted to punch him for the Wade remark, but...he *wanted* her to stay for himself?

She drew a breath for patience and to clear her brain. "First of all, I would not be going back to Wade. I would simply be going back to work where Wade happens to be. Secondly I...I'm so confused about us, I don't know *what* I want."

"It's not that confusing," he said. "We still love each other."

"Dillon, that's what's *causing* my confusion! I have—" She stopped abruptly, forcing the words back and starting over. "*You* have two little babies that belong to another woman. What if she comes back and wants the four of you to be a family?" She pointed toward the room where the babies slept, instinctively lowering her voice. "You love them. I know you do. And it would only be right that you all be together." How it hurt to say that.

"You're forgetting that she left them for me at the hospital," he said. "Does that sound to you like she wants them? I'm just trying to find her to confirm that they're mine. She and I would never be happy together."

"You made babies together. You may have to learn."

He drew a groaning breath and ran a hand over his face. "I don't see any reason why you and I can't raise them."

Harper sighed at the thought. That would be like having every prayer answered. But still, the pitfalls were enormous—and everywhere. "Well, then we're faced with the old problem of you being unwilling to settle down and stay closer to home. Just as you don't want me to stay if I'm just staying for the twins, I don't want you to marry me if you're just doing it so that there's someone around to care for them while you're racing across the globe."

He frowned over that, arms folded. When he looked up at her, his eyes were weary. "I didn't have every detail of the future worked out, yet. Just tell me. Are you staying or not?"

"Yes, I'm staying."

"For me?"

"For me. And thank you again for the desk. Good night."

DILLON WAS AMAZED that life could go on so smoothly with such ambivalence and uncertainty between Harper and him. In medicine, you had to get to the facts before you could act. In life, it seemed, you were forced to keep acting when you didn't really know what was happening—or where your actions would lead.

But life in the Dancer's Beach cottage moved ahead with a pleasant domesticity that completely surprised him. He and Harper fell into a usually comfortable routine with the twins, helping and supporting each other in a way that seemed to invalidate their personal disputes. It meant, he guessed, that they were good parents—but poor lovers.

In their spare time, they worked on the treasures in the garage. Harper had finished the trunk, which now sat on the floor at the foot of Dillon's bed, and in which she'd placed a second blanket and extra linens for his bathroom.

She'd finished stripping the dresser and night tables of the violent magenta, and was now staining the wood a rich gold oak.

He had rewired the lamp, found an amber glass tulip shade, and placed the light near her desk.

Another trip to Used But Enthused had yielded another pair of end tables that were maple, but in good repair and in need only of sanding and restaining. He put them in Darrick's room.

Harper brought him coffee Sunday afternoon, while he took the paint off an old window frame she'd talked him into buying.

"Thank you. What were we going to do with this again?" he asked her as he took the cup.

"I'm going to decorate it with moss, a few dried flowers and a little bird, and it's going to look great on a wall in the sunroom." She smiled brightly at him, and he thought that there were times when he didn't really care if he ever came to understand her, as long as she stayed with him. Then her eyes focused on something behind his head and they lit up with excitement—the way they used to do for him.

She ran past him through the open door of the garage and out to the street where a silver luxury sedan was pulling up to the curb.

Dillon muttered an expletive when the door opened and Wade stepped out, taking Harper into his arms.

Chapter Seven

Dillon felt an intense dislike for Wade Warren Winthrop. He was the kind of man every baseball-loving, jeans-wearing, sweat-bearing male hated, because he looked as though he'd never sat in the cheap seats, never wore anything without a designer label, and never did anything that put a hair out of place—and yet women loved him anyway.

It was impossible to trust a man like that.

Dillon had first met Winthrop when Harper brought him home with her after a photography seminar in Portland where each had conducted a workshop. They'd talked then about going into business together. Harper was working for the *Edenfield Signal* as a reporter-photographer at the time, and Winthrop was teaching photography in a community college near Seattle.

They'd eventually decided the start-up costs were too high, but continued to stay in touch. Dillon had always suspected that Winthrop had a sexual interest in Harper.

Harper insisted Dillon was crazy.

Now as Winthrop and Harper headed back toward him, arm in arm and laughing, Dillon quelled the fiery billow of belligerence inside him and wiped his hands on a rag. He didn't know what the man was doing here, but hoped he wouldn't be doing it long.

"Dillon," Harper said cheerfully as she and Winthrop walked into the garage. "I called Wade and asked him to FedEx my Hasselblad, but he decided to bring it himself. Wasn't that thoughtful?" The camera hung around her neck already.

Winthrop extended his hand toward Dillon, who met it with his own. "Very thoughtful," he said dutifully, detecting a look in Winthrop's eyes that said he wasn't thrilled to see him, either.

"I thought it was safer than shipping it." Winthrop moved around Dillon to admire the babies in their carrier. They were wide awake. He leaned close to them and gently chucked their chins with the pad of his index finger.

Two gummy smiles welcomed him.

Traitors, Dillon accused them silently. *This guy would never get up with you at night or let you drool on the shoulder of his shirt.*

They continued to smile, apparently considering those failings unimportant.

"Come and join us for coffee," Harper said to Dillon, picking up the carrier.

Winthrop took it from her. It was all Dillon could do to stop himself from yanking the carrier back. Instead he simply held up the full cup she'd just brought him. "Got some, thanks."

As Winthrop shamelessly talked baby-talk to the twins, Harper glared at Dillon. "I have scones inside. Please join us."

"I don't..." he began, but her eyes widened as though underlining a wordless threat. "I'll be right there," he said finally. "Soon as I finish the last side of this pane."

Dillon took his time, trying to tune out the laughter and eager conversation coming from the kitchen. He hung the frame on a nail to dry, carefully capped the solvent, put the rags he'd used into a metal can, then locked the garage door.

He washed his hands upstairs, scrubbing them as thoroughly as if he were preparing for surgery, changed his shirt and finally went down to the kitchen.

Harper and Winthrop sat at the kitchen table, poring over contact proofs. Dillon went to the counter to pour himself a cup of coffee. Winthrop placed an 8×12 in front of Harper; she put both hands over her eyes and shrieked with horrified laughter.

Dillon peered into the carrier on the edge of the table and saw that Michelle was fast asleep. Gabrielle grinned at him. He picked her up, settled her in his arm, then sat at a right angle to Harper.

"Incriminating photo?" he teased.

Harper continued to stare at it, a hand to her mouth.

"You could say that," Winthrop answered for her, pushing the photo away from Harper and toward Dillon.

"It was an ad we did for Guy Gifts, Inc.," he said. "The model we hired got a black eye that morning and called in, but we had to do the shoot because the tiger had already arrived."

Tiger? Dillon pulled the photo toward him and his eyes passed right over the tiger. All he saw was Harper in high-fashion makeup, the sides of her hair pulled up with combs for a sophisticated look, and nothing else on her body but a wide red ribbon wound around her and covering her only strategically. A bow was tied at her neck. The copy under the photo read, "Wrap up something special for the tiger in your life."

One breast was mostly concealed by the ribbon, but the soft swell of the underside of the other was clear, as was the flare of both hips.

Dragging his eyes from this vision, Dillon finally saw the tiger sitting up beside Harper and leaning docilely against her. He'd been caught in mid-yawn, except that it looked like mid-roar, his several inches long incisors showing.

He had to say something disparaging. "Great shot, but women are buying gifts for guys. Would a half-naked woman lure another woman into using Guy Gifts?"

Winthrop nodded amiably. "That was Harper's point when they first proposed the idea to us, but they insisted."

Dillon shrugged. "Ultimately the sales figures will tell the story."

Winthrop laughed. "True. In the meantime, Guy Gifts has ordered 50,000 poster-size copies of this photo to offer as bonus gifts. I understand they've already pre-sold a considerable number to their staff. I brought you a couple." He pulled a large envelope out of a portfolio leaning against his chair and passed it to Harper, who passed it on to Dillon.

She smiled tentatively at him, her expression half-horrified, half-hopeful. "What do you think?" she asked.

He swallowed all the hostile and jealous responses that gathered on his tongue. "What does Guy Gifts sell?" he asked, silently suggesting things that came in brown-paper wrappers.

"A wide variety of things," Winthrop replied seriously. "From personal items to office accessories."

Harper, catching Dillon's implication, turned back to study the photo critically. "I'm covered," she insisted a little weakly.

"If you weighed one more pound," Dillon said, "you wouldn't be."

Winthrop handed Harper a manila folder. "That was the point," he said to Dillon.

Dillon nodded and said with exaggerated courtesy, "You made it very well."

Harper gave Dillon an annoyed look, then opened the folder.

"That's as far as I've gotten with ideas for the Manchester Linens campaign. I was hoping we could brainstorm something more before I leave."

Harper leaned her forearms on the contents of the folder and faced Winthrop with the glow of excitement on her face. "I actually have some great ideas that involve the twins." She touched the carrier on the table. "Dillon's sister-in-law suggested it, and it seems like a natural. Their slogan is 'nursery soft' so it's built-in success to me. Can you stay the night so we can talk about it?"

Dillon watched Winthrop catch her enthusiasm. He found the connection between them deeply depressing; it was the click of mutual understanding he himself couldn't quite get again with her.

Winthrop glanced at Dillon, obviously aware that as far as Dillon was concerned, he wasn't welcome to spend the night.

Dillon decided that he couldn't blame Winthrop for his own inability to deal with Harper—though he'd have loved to have had somewhere else to plant the blame. He stood. "He can use Darrick's room," he said to Harper. "I'll go back to the garage and give you two some privacy." He picked up the carrier, prepared to take the babies with him.

Harper stopped him. "No, leave them with us," she said, holding the carrier down, then reaching up for Gabrielle. "They're our inspiration, after all. Do we have anything for dinner?"

"I'd like to take you all out to dinner," Winthrop offered.

Harper looked uncertain. "Thanks, Wade, but I don't know. Two little babies can destroy the ambience of any restaurant."

"Well, if it gets too bad we'll ask for doggie bags."

Harper looked to Dillon for a decision.

"Sure," he said, marveling at his own powers of cooperation. He hadn't known he had it in him.

Dillon spent the next few hours sanding the pew he'd removed from the kitchen and which Harper thought should go in the upstairs hall. It had intricate carved work on the sides that he attacked by hand with fine sandpaper.

When Harper walked into the garage, he was lying on the floor, his elbow propping up his head as he worked on the decorative ridge around the bottom. She climbed over him, and sat in the corner of the pew, hanging over it to watch him work.

"You ready to quit for dinner?" she asked.

He didn't look up at her. "Just give me about five minutes. Then I can be showered and changed in fifteen."

"I fed the girls," she said. "If all goes well, they should sleep while we eat."

"Dreamer."

"I know. I'm just hoping for the best." She leaned an arm over the side and poked his temple with her index finger. "I appreciate your being polite. I know you don't like him."

He moved the sandpaper gently over the center of a stylized flower, concentrating on the task without comment.

She poked his temple again. "He's really a very nice, very talented person."

"Uh-huh."

"There's nothing between us but business."

"Uh-huh."

"Dillon," she began impatiently, poking him again.

He caught her index finger and pulled her halfway over the side of the pew. "You poke me with that one more time," he threatened, feeling edgy and out of sorts, "and I'll sand it off for you."

He turned onto his back on the floor to support half her weight as she braced her hands on his shoulders.

"Well, you wouldn't look at me!" she complained.

"I'm looking at you now." He spoke testily, his hands holding her waist, her legs still caught on the pew. "What do you want?"

She parted her lips to tell him she'd just wanted to call him for dinner—but suddenly it wasn't about that at all. Suddenly the issue was everything that lay unresolved between them—the hot, deep love that had been elbowed aside by needs that made them incompatible.

She found herself desperately wanting a connection, a starting place, a moment of pure emotion that didn't need every little detail analyzed and every little problem solved.

She bent her arms to let herself fall toward him. At

the same moment, he pulled her the rest of the way off the pew, careful that she landed on his cushioning body.

And then she kissed him—or he kissed her. She wasn't entirely sure which. She only knew they were devouring each other, that her hands were in his hair and his hands were all over her—and she swore she heard the violent *whoosh* of ignition as all the feelings she'd tamped down lit up again.

She remembered this feeling, their old heat and passion and the absolute rightness of finding it in the arms of a soulmate. But there was a new dimension now that their old fire hadn't had: a new tenderness, a new wisdom that accepted more than it demanded.

The sudden sounds of a baby crying and an anxious voice saying, "I'm sorry, but..." brought them back to reality with a jolt. Both turned to the walkway where Winthrop stood with a screeching Michelle in his arms.

"I'm sorry," he said again, and to his credit he did look truly apologetic. "She won't stop crying, and I don't know what to do."

Harper scrambled hastily off Dillon's lap, ignoring the tenderness of his steadying arm. She went to take the baby, crooning to her guiltily. Then she hurried with her into the house.

Winthrop followed with another quick, embarrassed apology.

DILLON HAD A WHOLE NEW attitude about their guest. It was easier to be polite to him now, to engage him in conversation, because Winthrop had seen for himself where Harper's affections lay—literally.

That gave Dillon a sense of superiority that he tried not to flaunt, but that he was sure came through as the natural result of Harper's reaction to him—and Winthrop's firsthand witness of it.

Winthrop seemed a little less ebullient, a little less prone to put an arm around Harper, as had previously been his custom.

The twins slept through the restaurant meal, but Michelle, proving Harper's theory once again, apparently didn't want to miss dessert. Her fussing woke her sister, and Dillon took both babies into his arms, while Harper hurriedly polished off her dessert.

Downing the last of his wine, Winthrop looked Dillon over with what appeared to be grudging interest. Then he turned to Harper. "You should try a few shots of *him* holding the twins for the Manchester campaign. Maybe with a sheet thrown across him like a Scotsman wears his plaid. It'd get the female consumer."

"Mmm." There was speculation in Harper's voice, but she showed no real enthusiasm for the idea. Dillon thought he detected a decided lack of enthusiasm for him particularly.

But her lips had told him another story several hours earlier.

"I'd have to have union scale, of course," he said, taking a certain pleasure in looking into the face of Harper's ambivalence. She'd certainly caused him confusion enough times for him to feel justified in taking pleasure in hers. "And whatever a baby wrangler gets on a photo shoot."

Harper shook her head at him. "And I suppose you'd like your own chair with a big star on it."

He pretended interest. "Is that possible?"

Her eyes narrowed as she studied him and he could see that she'd suddenly caught Winthrop's vision.

"Maybe against a bank of pillows propped up to the headboard. And sheets and towels all over."

"Yeah." Winthrop studied Dillon in the same considering way. "And maybe one of him bare-chested, each baby wrapped in a towel as though she's just been bathed. That'd be a money-maker."

That jangled her out of the creative vision and she was just Harper, the woman, again, imagining Dillon bare-chested with babies. She blushed again guiltily.

Winthrop frowned at her. "Or will that just pose a threat to completion of the work?"

Harper looked from Dillon to Winthrop as though she didn't know what to make of either of them, then suggested they leave the restaurant.

"Wade and I still have work to do," she said, busily gathering up bottles and pacifiers. She stuffed the bottles into the diaper bag, but hooked the binkies on her index finger for quick availability. "And he'll have to get some sleep if he's leaving early in the morning."

She assumed control of the return home like a general marshaling troops. Even Winthrop looked a little concerned when she took his arm and pushed him into the front seat next to Dillon, then took the position near the door. With the babies relegated to the back for safety.

Once at home, she left Dillon in the living room with the wide-awake babies, and closed herself and Winthrop in the kitchen where all their work was still strewn across the table.

Dillon wandered in occasionally for formula for the babies or a cup of coffee for himself, and found them engrossed in their projects.

Winthrop was sprawled in his chair, his feet propped on an empty one. Harper knelt on her chair and leaned over the table, her pants-clad derriere a charming view from the refrigerator door.

They seemed to be in disagreement about a concept Winthrop was to present to a client the following week, and each time Dillon wandered into the kitchen, the argument seemed to be getting progressively more intense—at least on Harper's side.

Winthrop handled her with what appeared to be experienced calm, and when that didn't work, suddenly asked outright, "All right, what is it? What do you hate about it that you're not telling me?"

"I don't hate it, I like it!" she insisted in a hostile tone of voice.

"Then why are you shouting?"

"Because you're not listening to my ideas for the copy!"

"I'm listening, I just don't happen to agree!"

Dillon went back to the living room, coffee in hand, somewhat happy to see that someone else besides him had difficulty dealing with her.

Winthrop and Harper were still at work at the table when Dillon carried the sleeping twins up to bed at nine-thirty. He lay on the bed with a book, the sound of Harper's laughter catching his attention. Evidently Winthrop had managed to placate her. What was his secret?

He turned his light off after eleven and left his door slightly ajar.

Only a few minutes later he heard footsteps on the stairs, then Harper's voice saying quietly, "Bathroom's right across the hall. I think you'll find everything you need. We're right at the end."

"Great," Winthrop replied. "Thank you. You're okay about the presentation?"

"Sure. It was no big problem, I guess I'm just a little testy."

"That's all right. I understand. You always get in a flap when you get emotional about something you think you should be able to deal with logically."

"Like what?"

"You tell me. Twin babies? A demanding lover?"

There was a moment's silence, then she said, "Good night, Wade. We'll be up to fix your breakfast." Footsteps came farther up the hall and Dillon listened for the sound of her walking into her room.

He was surprised an instant later when his door opened farther and Harper walked into the bedroom. She closed the door behind her with a decisive click—as though she'd intended someone else to hear the sound.

Dillon propped up on an elbow, interested to know what her sudden intrusion meant. Not that he considered her presence an intrusion, but she'd always carefully avoided his room except when dealing with the babies.

She tiptoed in, apparently thinking him asleep and unable to see in the dark that he wasn't. She sat at the foot of the bed.

He nudged her bottom with his toe and she yelped, getting to her feet.

"Ssh!" he teased. "He'll think there're acrobatics going on in here. Or is that the idea?"

"You, ssh!" she returned, walking halfway up the side of the bed. He judged by her careful steps that her eyes still weren't adjusted to the dark. "I just need—"

He homed in on the sound of her voice, reached for her shadowy form and caught her wrist. He yanked her onto the bed, and she fell in a sprawl over him. Then he tipped her onto her side and into the curve of his arm.

He could feel the same irritable restlessness in her that she'd displayed with Winthrop all evening.

"You just need...what?" he asked. Her breath came in rapid gasps and her hair was under his nose, in his mouth. The moment was suddenly heart-stoppingly familiar. Only he remembered her drawing him closer instead of pushing him away.

"To...stay here for a few minutes," she whispered breathlessly.

"All right." Her hair was a bright tangle in the darkness. He brushed it out of her face and tucked it behind her ear. She looked and felt like glowing ivory silk.

She went still suddenly, and the darkness became a cocoon around them. Velvety. Hot. All-encompassing.

"Don't you want to know why?" she whispered after a moment.

"I'd rather let my imagination run wild," he whispered back.

"I told him we were sleeping together."

"My imagination's on target, then."

She punched a halfhearted little fist against his chest. "He was making romantic moves on me. I think because he saw you kissing me. I had to do something. He's taking a shower. In a few minutes he'll go back to his room, and I can go back to mine."

Not exactly the fulfillment of Dillon's fantasies. "And I'm just expected to cooperate."

She sighed and her fist against his chest opened out to pat him in apology. "I know I'm being selfish, but it would help me a lot if you would."

Selfish? This was the sweetest few minutes he'd had in two years, except for the anniversary party.

"All right." He settled her onto her left side and curled his body around hers, pillowing her head on his left arm and wrapping the other one around her. "We may as well be comfortable while we wait."

He felt her weight against him, the small snuggle of her head, the stretch of a leg that he knew meant she was relaxing.

"Thanks, Dillon."

"Sure."

She was asleep before Winthrop finished his shower. Dillon heard the water stop running, the quiet buzz of something electrical that he suspected was a blow-dryer, then the quiet opening and closing of doors as Winthrop went back to his room—Darrick and Skye's room.

Harper would sleep for hours. Dillon recognized the exhaustion in her. Over the last week she'd been up with the babies often, and during the day she'd done her share of cooking, dishes, laundry, as well as spending every spare moment working on the furniture in the garage.

And the state of their relationship itself was wearing—he was aware of it himself all the time. It was hard to have deep feelings for someone and know that nothing could be done about them until several issues were resolved—issues that centered on people who couldn't be found and emotional knots Freud himself would find difficult to undo.

So he held her close—thankful for the moment—and closed his eyes.

Chapter Eight

Harper opened her eyes to darkness and knew instantly
that something was wrong. No, not wrong but...what?
Off-kilter, out of rhythm?

She wondered if some natural disaster had taken
place while she slept.

Slept. She didn't remember going to bed. Maybe that
was the problem. She'd walked upstairs with Wade,
shown him to his room, walked down the hall to her
own...

And that was when it all came back.

She became aware of the snug harbor of Dillon's
body where she lay. She was completely surrounded
by him, held tightly against him. Safe. Secure.

It was as though he held her entire being in the safe
circle of his arms—as though he protected her pride,
her dreams, her fears, her ambitions. He took them as
his own and shielded them from a world that sometimes lacked compassion or even understanding.

God, she missed that.

And then it occurred to her that at that moment, at
least, she had it. It was hers. In this shadowy room in
Dancer's Beach with the surf pounding outside and
moonlight silvering the windows, he sheltered her.

And suddenly she knew what had awakened her. The tension in the room was palpable.

"Dillon?" she whispered.

A second passed. "Yeah?" he asked.

"You're awake."

Another second passed. "Yeah."

"Can't sleep?"

"Don't want to," he said.

She turned in his arms. "Why not?"

He ran his hand gently up and down her spine. "Because it's been a long time since I've had you quiet in my arms. I didn't want to miss a second of it."

She looped her arms around his neck and used them to pull herself up so that she could look into his face. His eyes were bright in the darkness.

She wasn't sure where the courage came from, unless it was the magical intimacy of the middle-of-the-night quiet, but she asked, "Do you love Allison Cartier?"

He shook his head. "No, I don't."

"Does she love you?"

"No."

She braced herself to tell him what she should have told him long ago, except that the truth posed so many problems she hadn't felt strong enough to deal with.

But she felt as though she knew him better now, knew herself better.

She put her hand to his face and started with, "*I* love you, Dillon." Her lips were a centimeter away from his. "I love you so much. I want—"

His lips pinned her to the pillow while his hands swept over her, assessing what she wore, dispensing with it.

She surfaced from a kiss that threatened to knot her

vocal chords, to find that she was without shirt and bra and that he was yanking her pants and panties from her and tossing them aside.

"Dillon," she whispered, reason fluttering away as his hands stroked over her bare flesh for the first time in almost a year.

Shudders of sensation ran under her skin in the wake of his touch up her thigh, over her stomach, to her waist.

She said his name again, but he didn't hear her because she was too breathless to create sound.

He'd turned her onto her stomach and she felt him kneel astride her. She inhaled the fragrance of his aftershave, of wood stain, and of the imprint of some scent that was uniquely, elusively Dillon. His hands reached under her to take her small breasts into his palms. She felt his cheek beside hers, his lips at her ear. "I love you, Harper," he said softly, punctuating the statement with a kiss. "There are no words to tell you what my life's been like without you."

His thumbs moved gently over the very tips of her breasts and sensation shot through her, bouncing from place to place, centering at the warm, moist heart of her. Everything else fled her mind.

His lips moved to the back of her neck, along the lines of her shoulders, down the middle of her back, planting a kiss on every vertebra. She gripped the pillowcase in both fists as the little shudders of anticipation began.

He kissed the base of her spine, the backs of her thighs, the hollows of her knees.

Desperate to be able to touch him, Harper turned onto her back, clasped her hands behind his neck and pulled him down to her.

He laughed softly, planting a kiss at her throat. "I wasn't finished with you yet."

"I was anxious to participate myself," she said, remembering how he reacted to the light strum of her fingernails.

He groaned into her hair as she ran them over his back and down his side, wedged a space between their bodies to stroke over his pectoral muscles and his stomach.

"You were going to get your chance." His voice was a little strained.

"I wasn't prepared to wait."

"That's because you're a brat, accustomed to having your..."

Her hands closed possessively over his manhood and as she felt his entire body react, she asked, "I'm a *what?*"

"An angel!" he capitulated quickly. "A fallen one sometimes, but an angel nonetheless."

He parted her thighs, claiming her womanhood with the tender authority of a man who loved her. Suddenly the struggle for control of the encounter ended with the race for unity.

He entered her, she wrapped her legs around him in welcome, and time seemed to stop to give love the space it needed. Nothing moved or beat or ticked. Past and future fused into the present. Everything they'd been to each other, everything they dreamed of being came together in what they gave to and took from each other.

When their lovemaking ended, Harper wept.

"I don't want to lose us again," she whispered, her voice thick.

He kissed her temple and held her more tightly. "We'll solve everything. I promise you."

Harper knew he meant it, but as he settled her against his shoulder and wiped her tears away with his thumb, she realized that however well-intentioned, she'd created a situation even he couldn't easily fix. And his having twins with Allison Cartier was only half of it.

The easy half.

SHE ANSWERED THE TELEPHONE the following morning just after Wade drove off for Seattle. A very British female voice told her that she represented CDN and wanted to speak to Dillon.

She went to the kitchen door to shout for him. He was in the garage, staining the pew.

"CDN," she said quietly as he took the receiver from her. The babies lay on the counter within his reach, both wide awake. He made eyes at them while he waited, keeping his stained hands out to his sides.

"Yes," he said finally. "This is McKeon. Oh, hi, Barney. Yeah. Any news?" He listened. "Isn't that a long time? I mean, are you sure she's all right?" Another pause. "They did? Well, that's good. But no idea when she'll be back? Yeah. No, I know. When she's on to something she forgets the rest of the world exists. Or she remembers, and that's why she considers it so important. Yeah, thanks. Right. Bye."

Harper poured Dillon a cup of coffee to take back to the garage with him. "No sign of her yet?"

"No." Dillon smiled at the babies and got wide smiles back, then he turned to Harper. "But they're in touch with the man who set up the meeting for her, and he insists that she's fine."

"But they don't know when she'll be back?"

"No." Dillon took the coffee she handed him in one hand, then put the other arm around her and drew her close. "You all right this morning?"

Physically she was fine, though they'd awakened again in the wee hours of the morning and made love until dawn. Emotionally, she was about to blow a gasket—whatever that was.

The last two weeks with Dillon had reminded her how special he was—and last night had reminded her that he could also be absolutely magnificent. She couldn't imagine a woman walking away from him—particularly when he was in possession of her babies.

But that seemed to be what had happened. There was just a question of whether or not the situation was permanent. It was entirely possible that Allison Cartier had gone to Edenfield to have her babies, wanting to be near Dillon's family until he returned from Nicaragua.

By some fluke of fate, Darrick had been away at a conference. Then she probably received last-minute confirmation of the meeting she'd been trying so long to set up and, driven woman that she was, left the twins in the care of the hospital until her return.

Harper frowned as reexamination of that theory revealed too many holes.

"I'm fine," she lied, wrapping her arms around him and holding him tightly. She had to talk to him now—today. But she had no idea how to broach the subject. *Darling? Don't be upset, but you're in even more trouble than you think you are.* or *Dillon, I have some life-altering news.*

No. The poor man was worried enough about the twins' mother as it was. She went to another subject entirely. "I wonder if anybody's heard from Duncan."

"Mom would have called."

She raised her head to smile at him. "Your parents are in Vegas, remember? Probably taking in the Folies Bergère and developing slots-players' elbow."

Dillon laughed. "That would be better than if they were haunting antique shops."

"About the horse collar with the clock in it..."

"Darrick said they sent it from San Diego when Darrick and Skye had been here only a couple of days. Skye made him put it in a place of honor."

Harper giggled. "Their horrid taste in old things is part of their charm. The important thing is that they thought it was wonderful and wanted their sons to have it."

"That's what Skye said."

"You're very lucky to belong to this group, you know."

"You don't have to tell me that." He kissed her forehead. "I'll be finished with the pew in another half hour. You want to go living room furniture shopping this afternoon? We have most of our projects finished."

"Sounds like a plan."

"Good. I'll buy you lunch."

"But the babies..."

"Dinner worked out the other night. We might get lucky again."

As it turned out, Harper reflected later, that was the point at which her luck ran out.

WHILE DILLON SHOWERED and changed, she packed the diaper bag and stuffed it into the bottom of the stroller on the front porch. She was happy with their new relationship and thought it might be strong enough now to bear the strain of the truth. But later. Tonight, maybe.

As she turned back to the house to carry the twins out, she heard a car pull into the driveway behind her.

She felt instant panic when she recognized her aunt Cleo's car. She ran to it, certain something was desperately wrong.

Then she saw the child seat in the back, and Darian sitting up brightly, reaching his hands toward her excitedly as she opened the old car's back door.

She also thought later how inexplicable it was that though the past two years of her life had turned on the need to keep her son's existence secret, she forgot all that that morning in her concern over his well-being.

Cleo got out of the car and rushed around it to hover nearby, explaining her sudden appearance, as Harper pulled her fifteen-month-old son out of his car seat.

"I'm sorry, sweetie," Cleo said hurriedly. "I know you've got your hands full here, but I didn't know what else to do. Phyl and Aggie are off on a cruise, and Edie and Grace are nowhere to be found!"

Harper straightened, hugging the baby to her, trying to make sense of her aunt's words while dealing with her own excitement at seeing her child for the first time in two weeks.

Darian clung to her neck. "Ma-ma!" he said excitedly.

"I know I begged you to leave him with me, but you won't believe what's happened!"

"A man?" Harper guessed. Cleo had been married and divorced twice. She was the tallest of the sisters, always chicly dressed, with short gray hair in a fashionable cut. The second husband, a race car driver, had given her a very comfortable settlement.

Cleo dismissed that possibility with a scornful wave of her hand. "A publisher!" she corrected excitedly.

For as long as Harper could remember, Cleo had been working in her spare time on a novel about a sisters quintet. It was half murder mystery, half biography/saga of the Stratton Sisters.

"You're kidding!"

"No! Prather Books wants to buy *Night After Night*, but they want some changes and asked if I could get to L.A. to talk about them. They publish a lot of things about Hollywood."

"Cleo!"

"I know! I'm so excited I can hardly stand it. I tried to call you, but you were out and I didn't want to leave the news of my first literary sale on an answering machine!"

"Of course." Harper tried to tug her toward the house. "Come in and take a break. Have a cup of coffee…"

Cleo shook her head. "My flight leaves from Portland in two and a half hours, so I'll just be on my way and try to relax when I get to the airport."

Harper hugged her tightly. "Good luck, Auntie. I'm *so* proud of you. And thanks for taking care of Daredevil for me."

Cleo kissed Darian's cheek. "He was a doll. We had a great time. Bye, sweetie. I'll call you when I get home." Then Cleo raised her eyes beyond Harper, smiled broadly and waved. "Hi, Dillon! Gotta run! Harper will explain!" She blew him a kiss.

Harper turned to see Dillon standing in the doorway, and that was when she realized what had just happened.

Or, rather, what was about to happen.

Dillon returned Cleo's wave as she backed out of

the driveway and drove off with a tap of her horn. But his eyes never left Harper and the toddler in her arms. There was a tense speculation in his bearing.

He was counting months, she was sure—calculating when they'd broken up almost two years ago, probably thinking *a nine-month pregnancy, and a baby a little over a year old.*

Still, it might occur to him that Darian could have resulted from a liaison she'd had just after she and Dillon had parted—except that he had the McKeon stamp on him as clearly as if he wore a sign. His hair was very dark, and he already had Dillon's frank expression, his easy laughter, and that same need to be always on the move.

Darian kicked his little feet now, and Harper set him down. He ran toward Dillon, who stood on the top of the porch. He'd set down the carrier with the twins in it and now stared at the toddler coming toward him.

Heart in her throat, Harper stayed right behind her son. He was fairly good with stairs, but climbing them was still a project for his sturdy but very short legs.

Darian tackled one step at a time on all fours, eagerly, fearlessly, aiming for the top.

But as he approached, he found the large man sitting on the porch, his feet on the third step down. Uninhibited, Darian used Dillon's shoes, then the leg of his jeans, then his knee to pull himself upward.

For the final step, Dillon offered his hand and Darian took it. Darian reached the porch with a squeal of excitement, stamping his feet in victory.

Then he noticed the twins in the carrier and leaned over them, squealing again. He pointed a small finger at them and said something indecipherable to Harper.

She smiled and nodded, almost unable to breathe. "Babies," she said.

He turned his focus to Dillon. They were now eye to eye, and they stared at each other.

Harper waited, halfway up the steps, feeling as though she might die of the tension.

Darian, accustomed to love and admiration from her, her aunts, Wade, and everyone else who crossed his path, threw a stubby little leg over Dillon's thigh and sat down, facing him.

Dillon put an arm around him to steady him and looked up into Harper's eyes. The question was gone out of his gaze and was replaced by the knowledge that he was holding his son. There was amazement, incredulity, awe—and a fury so dark that Harper had to wonder if she'd just lost everything.

"What's his name?" he asked stiffly.

She swallowed before she replied. "Darian," she said. "Aunt Cleo calls him Dare-devil."

At the sound of his name, the toddler turned to her.

Dillon studied the bright little face, then looked up at her again, anger now emanating from him like a sound wave.

"Were you just going to invite me to his graduation in twenty years?" he asked coldly.

"Dillon..." She prepared to explain, not at all sure how she intended to do that, but he stood abruptly, swinging Darian onto his hip, and started down the stairs.

She followed him, worried about his frame of mind. "Dillon, please..."

He turned and held a hand out to stop her. Darian held on to his shoulder and watched him with a little frown.

"Don't come near me," Dillon ordered quietly. "Or I won't be responsible."

Darian leaned out of his arms and reached for Harper. "Ma-ma!" he said.

"Dillon, he's frightened," she pleaded, taking another step toward him.

"Whose fault is that?" Dillon asked, pulling the toddler back toward him. "He doesn't know who I am!"

"Dill—"

He shook his head to silence her. "We're leaving," he said and headed down the walk.

She followed to the edge of the lawn. "Where are you going? He doesn't have a sweater!"

But they were already across the road and headed for the beach. Sobbing, Harper hurried back to the twins, now fussing in the carrier, and went back into the house with them.

Michelle and Gabrielle picked up her tension and her tears and fussed all afternoon. She tried rocking them, bathing them, propping them up against pillows on the sofa—while she paced from window to window, looking for some sign of Dillon and Darian's return.

The girls finally ate late in the afternoon and drifted off to sleep.

She tried to think about preparing something for dinner, but she had a suspicion her son and his father would not be home for it. And *she* couldn't have eaten if she'd wanted to.

So she made a pot of tea and prowled the quiet house. She made herself consider what might result from that morning's events.

She'd kept Darian a secret because she knew how the McKeons were about family. And since she and

Dillon found it impossible to live together, she hadn't wanted her son to live his life in split custody.

So she'd assured her aunts that she'd told Dillon and his family about him. With her in Seattle and the McKeons in Oregon and California, the secret had been easily kept.

Until now.

She felt awash with regret. She'd been wrong to keep the secret, but she'd thought herself justified.

This time with Dillon and the twins, however, had showed her what a good father he could be. She felt sorry that her son had missed being with him.

And now she also knew that though she'd gotten on with her life, she hadn't gotten over Dillon—would never be over him. And though it had looked as though he wanted her to remain in his life once he'd found the twins' mother, she felt sure that was no longer the case.

She imagined a custody dispute, lawyers, horrified family on both sides.

She went to the front window as she had a hundred times since night had fallen, and wondered anxiously where Dillon and Darian could be. It never crossed her mind that Dillon would harm his son, but she wouldn't put it past him to want to hurt *her*.

Was he hiding him away somewhere right now?

Even as she began to experience renewed panic, a cab pulled into the driveway. In the glow from the porchlight, she saw Dillon alight from the cab, Darian asleep on his shoulder.

The cabdriver got out, opened the trunk, and helped ferry into the house a tricycle, a rocking horse, a giant bear and a shopping bag filled with smaller toys.

Harper opened the door to help and was not surprised when Dillon—the sleeping Darian in one arm, the bright red plastic trike in the other—walked in without saying a word to her.

The cabdriver was courteous though, and complimented her on her beautiful son before he left.

Harper had put the babies to sleep on Peg and Charlie's bed so she could hear them, and Dillon went to check on them, still carrying Darian.

Harper tucked the toys into a corner of the living room and went to make a pot of coffee for Dillon and to microwave her last cup of tea. She felt great relief that they were back but enormous trepidation over the coming confrontation.

Finally satisfied that Michelle and Gabrielle were comfortably asleep, Dillon reemerged with Darian and lay him down on the old settee.

Harper delved into the bag Cleo had returned with him and found a diaper and cotton-footed pajamas. She offered them to Dillon, who took them without a word.

Darian, she noted, was wearing new overalls, and a minute leather bomber jacket. Dillon wore a dark-blue sweatshirt he hadn't had on when he'd left.

When he finally joined her at the table, her nerves were as tight as a bowstring, and though she knew he had every right to his anger, she was now feeling some pretty powerful stuff herself.

He pulled his chair back from the table and sank slowly into it as though exhausted. In spite of everything, she felt herself wanting to smile. He'd apparently had a taste of how lively a kinetic one-year-old could be compared to two still fairly immobile infants.

But he looked no less angry than he had when he'd left.

He took a sip of coffee, leaned back in his chair and

said simply, "I presume there's an explanation. I'd like to hear it."

She might have taken exception to his approach, but she realized she had very few cards to play here. And there were babies asleep on either side of the kitchen, so she had to keep her indignation down.

She drew a breath and tried to sound calm and conciliatory without appearing shamefaced and defeated—not an easy feat when that was much closer to how she felt.

"I didn't know I was pregnant," she explained, "until a couple of weeks after we'd broken up. I called your office to try to see you, but Janie told me you'd gone fishing with your dad and brothers. I didn't want to break that up, so I waited. Then you went directly to some flood or earthquake or something and the longer it took to reach you, the more I began to realize that we weren't going to be able to come to any kind of compromise over our baby except his having to spend half his life with you and the other half with me, as though he were two people. I didn't want that for him."

She held his angry stare and went on. "So I kept it to myself."

She sighed, remembering her lovable aunt barging into the middle of her idyllic morning. "But the aunts were always on me about telling you, so I let them believe that I had. Cleo didn't know—when she brought Darian to me—that you didn't know about him."

He looked away from her, obviously struggling to remain calm. "And even after last night," he said, his voice strained, "you weren't going to tell me if Cleo hadn't shown up?"

Suddenly, she lost it. This was the part he'd never understood. "There was nothing different about last night, Dillon!" she shouted at him. It wasn't true, but she wanted to hurt him. He'd forced her to live without him and now he was making *her* the villain? "We've always made wonderful, magical love, but that's never changed the outcome of our relationship. You still leave—and I still hate it!"

He stared at her in disbelief. "You're blaming *me* for the fact that you never told me I had a son?"

Dillon couldn't believe his ears. In fact, it had taken him the last twelve hours to believe his eyes!

She stared back at him, then shook her head. Her shoulders slumped and the display of temper was over as quickly as it had begun. "Dillon, I don't blame you for anything. Except maybe an heroic, active sperm count. I was wrong, I admit it. I should have told you. But every reason that held me back still exists like closed doors between us."

He nodded, more than willing to concede the point. "That's true. But you're as much at fault as I am, so I don't see why *I* have to be the one deprived of Darian."

She looked a little panicky and pointed toward the bedroom. "Dillon, you have two little girls..."

"And you think," he interrupted her, "that I'd cheerfully give up one of my children because I have two others?"

She looked heavenward imploringly. "No, I don't think that, but he's a very smart and happy little boy and I don't want to do anything to upset that."

He nodded again. "I don't see why anything has to. We'll see a lawyer and get joint custody worked out."

"And what happens if you have him and you get called to some emergency?"

He was quiet for the space of a heartbeat. That *was* going to be a problem and definitely something that might require some changes in his life. But he was still too angry with her to let her know that. "I'll make arrangements."

"What?" she demanded. "A nanny you keep on call? Dori's not going to be around until he's twenty-one, you know."

"Like she's been around at all."

"Dillon, this is serious. You don't love the twins' mother, and she left them at the hospital, so chances are you're going to be dealing with *them* alone. And you want to add a toddler to that?"

He knew it would be difficult, but he was feeling good about his ability to cope with the twins, and he and Darian had had fun together. "He's mine," he insisted.

"No, he's *ours*," she corrected. "And babies aren't about possession. They're about love and care and patience."

"Yes. And I think having them is usually about sharing them with their father." Then he added firmly, threateningly, and mostly for effect, "That's what the law says."

She burst to her feet. "The law?!" she shouted, fear visible in her anger. "You're threatening me with the law? You might consider how a judge will react to your fathering babies all over the place without benefit of marriage!"

She was right, but that only made him fire back in kind. "Probably the same way he'd react to thousands of posters of you wearing nothing but a wide ribbon being delivered by a place called Guy Gifts.''

She began to sputter a rebuttal but was too angry to be coherent. She finally went to the loveseat to pick up Darian, cradled him to her and stormed upstairs.

When Dillon heard her bedroom door close, he pushed himself to his feet and went around the house turning off the coffeepot and the lights, locking windows and doors.

His anger had subsided somewhat, but he was still in no mood to be conciliatory. He hated that Harper had withheld from him the knowledge of their bright and beautiful son, and he hated even more that he almost understood why she'd done it.

Almost. It was hard to accept that she hadn't understood that he'd have done whatever she'd wanted in order to be a part of Darian's life.

So, now he had three children: a son, and twin daughters.

He went into the bedroom to get the twins—and felt an unforgivably prideful need to strut.

DILLON AWOKE THE FOLLOWING morning to a storm in full temper outside, and the sound of babies crying somewhere downstairs. Beyond his window, rain fell from a mean-looking sky, and the wind howled.

The events of the night before came instantly to mind, but he couldn't summon the anger he'd felt then. He was still hurt that Harper had thought so little of him, but that didn't matter at this point. They had to find a way to move on from here.

He ran into the bathroom to brush his teeth and flipped on the light, but nothing happened. He flipped the switch again. Still nothing.

The storm had apparently knocked out electrical power. He remembered the Realtor warning him and his brothers when they bought the house that summer storms were a once- or twice-yearly occurrence here, and that power could be out for several days.

Fortunately they didn't have to worry about staying warm, although the big house might get a little drafty for the babies. He wondered if that was why they were crying.

Dillon ran to the kitchen and found the babies in their carrier on the counter, an extra blanket thrown over them. They weren't protesting the cold, he realized, but the unaccustomed lack of attention, as Harper ignored their cries and stuffed wood into the old enamel stove.

Darian, clutching the big bear Dillon had bought him the day before, ran to him as he walked into the room. He had a sweatshirt on over his pajamas.

Dillon picked him up and listened attentively as he pointed to the woodstove Harper worked over, spouting sounds that defied translation.

Harper looked frustrated but almost relieved to see him when he came up beside her.

"Thank God, you're up," she said, dusting her hands off and sitting back on her heels. "The power's out and I wanted to light the stove before it gets chilly in here. I expected to have hot water for tea going by the time you got down, and maybe even bacon and eggs underway, but I don't seem to be able to get the damn thing lit."

He set Darian on his feet and peered into the stove, wondering if this meant she, too, was willing to forget last night and try to find a way to make peace.

On the chance that that was the case, he was careful

not to laugh as he removed the wood from the oven. "That's because," he said gently, "you put the wood in the oven rather than in the firebox."

She made a self-deprecating face. "So I was going to bake wood?"

He patted her shoulder before placing kindling in the box, then stacking the wood. "No, because there'd have been nothing in the firebox to start it baking. You'd just have aged wood. See if you can get the girls quiet, and Darian and I'll get breakfast. And why don't you call the Fishers and see if they have provisions for fixing breakfast without power. If not, they're welcome to join us."

The Fishers did have a small generator, but asked whether if they brought pink grapefruit and Bertie's homemade bread for toast they could accept the offer anyway.

Breakfast turned into an all-day party. The Fishers were surprised by Darian's presence, but accepted Harper's brief explanation courteously and without further question.

"We have to call your parents," Harper said quietly to Dillon as he cooked.

"They won't be home until tomorrow," he replied. "I'll take care of it."

She was clearly confused by his cooperation. "I'll do it," she said after a moment. "I...should do it."

He felt as confused by her acceptance of the responsibility. "All right," he agreed.

Bertie entertained the twins, while Harper cleaned up, Darian playing with bowls and spoons beside her. Cliff insisted on helping Dillon carry the pew to the upstairs hall.

When the twins fell asleep on a blanket in a corner

of the sofa, Bertie handed Harper a plastic bag that contained an old embroidered pillowcase in which she'd stored what appeared to be a length of old silk. "A present for you," Bertie said.

Harper pulled the folded fabric out of the pillowcase, then opened it out, holding it beyond Darian's interested reach. It had yellowed with age to precisely the ivory color manufacturers tried to achieve with modern fabrics.

"It's gorgeous!" Harper exclaimed.

"Isn't it?" Bertie, sitting on the loveseat, leaned against the arm and nodded. "My mother had it from the time I was a little girl, so it's probably from the twenties or older. She bought it, intending to make an evening dress with it, but claimed she got too old to wear white before she ever got the project started. I thought you might be able to make baptismal dresses for the babies, or something."

"You're sure you can't use it?"

"I'm sure. Peg told me you were good with a needle."

"Moderately." Harper studied the shimmering fabric another moment, then folded it again. Thinking about having the babies baptized reminded her that it would be difficult to do that without knowing for certain who their mother was, and *that* brought to mind issues she didn't want to think about when it was turning into such a wonderful day—despite the storm and the loss of power.

She replaced the fabric in the pillowcase, then went to hug Bertie. "Thank you. I love it."

"It's so nice to have you kids for neighbors." Bertie grinned. "And your rotating residence certainly keeps the neighborhood fresh." She gathered Darian into her arms. "It's wonderful to have babies around, too. And this place is coming together. You wouldn't believe what it used to look like."

"Yellow and lavender, so Skye tells me."

"Yes. And it had been empty for a while, so it was pretty grim. But you kids have done wonders." She pointed to the horse-collar clock, shook her head and laughed richly. "Charlie and Peg are such a kick. Can you imagine finding that in a shop and actually wanting to give it to someone—someone you *love?*"

Harper laughed, too. "You should see some of the other things they've sent the boys. But the boys display them all because they appreciate the love behind their gifts—if not the good taste."

Bertie smiled. "Have you heard from Darrick and Skye? Skye developed quite an interest in the Buckley family while she was here." She pointed above their heads. "She showed me the dress form and the mirror upstairs."

"Yes." Harper experienced a little shiver along her scalp every time she thought of it. It wasn't fear, exactly, but an eerie sense of disorientation in finding herself in the presence of something—or some*one*—who wasn't real. "Now Skye's passed on the investigation to me. But I'm stuck. Unless you know what Olivia looked like."

Bertie frowned. "I don't. Why? Don't tell me you have a picture."

"I do—maybe." Harper took Fran's brown manila envelope and sat beside Bertie on the loveseat. Darian climbed into her lap, while Bertie took out and studied the ribbon, the hairpin, the receipt, the recipe, then lingered over the photos.

Over Bertie's shoulder, Harper admired the sweet

face of the woman in the photograph of the couple dressed for a ball, the look of happy surprise as though she couldn't quite believe her good fortune.

Darian reached for the photo, but Harper drew his hand back.

"Barton Buckley," Bertie said.

"I know. And isn't the woman lovely?"

Bertie tipped her glasses farther down on her nose and held the photo at arm's length as she tilted her head back to study it.

"She is."

"But her face isn't familiar to you?"

"No."

Harper sighed, dispirited. "I was hoping you'd be able to tell me it was Olivia, and that our theory that Barton followed her to the Klondike, found her and married her was substantiated."

Bertie handed back the photo, a slight smile on her face. "I can't tell you it's Olivia, but I can tell you who it isn't."

"Who isn't it?" Harper demanded.

"It isn't India, Barton's wife."

Chapter Nine

Dillon prepared steaks for lunch, since they were thawing in the useless freezer anyway, and Harper made salad to accompany them. Bertie and Cliff played with Darian and the girls in the living room.

Harper wanted to reestablish peace between her and Dillon. He didn't seem to be angry, but he was carefully cool. And after the warmth they'd shared before Cleo arrived with Darian, it made her feel as though a lid had been placed on her world, snuffing out the air, the life.

She reached into the cupboard over his head for the pepper.

He stepped aside to give her room—or to avoid her touch; she wasn't sure which.

"I'm sorry I didn't tell you about Darian," she blurted.

He turned to her, his expression difficult to read, then concentrated on the steaks again. "It's done," he said simply.

"I suppose you think my wanting to stay in one place seems like hiding," she went on, "but after the childhood I had, I need that. And I want it for Darian."

"But he's half me, Harp," he said. "He might want more than that."

"Okay, maybe. Eventually. But now he's a baby and he needs routine and security." She leaned against the counter so that she could look into Dillon's eyes. "What if...you took him on vacations and for...trips with your family." Her voice grew strained. "I'd like him to know your family."

He knew she was offering an olive branch, but he didn't think that particular arrangement was something he could agree to.

"Do you really think," he asked in a low voice, "that having a part-time father will make him feel secure? Particularly now that he knows me?"

"Dill, he doesn't *know* you," she said a little impatiently, not liking the direction this conversation was taking. "You've spent one evening together where you bought him all kinds of—"

And then, as though he'd been coached, Darian ran into the kitchen, wrapped an arm around Dillon's knee, and said very clearly and emphatically, "Da-da."

Harper put a hand to her hip. "You taught him to say that."

"Damn right I did." He reached a hand down to ruffle Darian's hair.

THE FISHERS WENT HOME just before dinner, though Dillon assured them they were welcome to stay. Bertie and Dillon had made spaghetti sauce, stew and seasoned chicken breasts to use up the rest of the meat that had thawed.

Dillon sent half of everything home with them.

"Maybe we'll get lucky," he said to Harper, "and the power will come on tonight so we can put all the

recooked dishes back in the freezer. Or at least keep it
for a few days in the refrigerator. This would be a good
time for my family to visit so they could eat up all this
stuff.''

"I wish we had tortillas to make chicken fajitas,"
Harper said longingly. She held Michelle in her arms
while Darian beat a plastic bowl with a wooden spoon.

Dillon wore Gabrielle in her front pack while covering the food he'd prepared. "We have flour and water," he said, reaching into a lower cupboard for the
bag. "I'll make them from scratch."

"I thought flour and water made glue," she challenged.

He shook his head at her in amused pity. "Maybe
when you cook. When I cook, they make great tortillas."

And they did. Dillon and Harper ate fajitas by can-
dlelight on the living room floor, with the babies sleeping cooperatively between them on their blanket. Even
Darian curled up and went to sleep in Dillon's arm.

The wind and the rain were finally abating, but there
was still no power.

"I'll sleep down here tonight with the twins," Dillon
said when it was time for bed, "so that I can keep the
fire going. You take Darian up to bed with you."

She'd have preferred to stay down here with him,
even in sleeping bags, but he clearly didn't want her—
and there was no point in fighting it.

He followed her upstairs, handed her the flashlight
from his truck, then carried down the portable crib.

As Harper put Darian in the middle of her bed and
quickly changed into a nightgown to join him, she
heard Dillon add more wood to the fire. She cuddled
her son to her and went to sleep.

She awoke shortly after midnight to loud screams in her ear.

Darian!

She reached for the bedside light, but it didn't respond to the switch. Of course. The power was still out.

She groped blindly for the flashlight, slid the switch, and found Darian standing by the bed, his face purple with the violence of his distress.

She pulled him back into bed with her and enfolded him in her arms, certain he was frightened about waking up in an unfamiliar place.

"It's okay, Dare-devil," she crooned, trying to rock him. "Mommy's here. It's okay."

But he pushed at her, climbed laboriously off the bed again, and tried to pull her with him.

"Dare, it's all right." She tried to catch him again, but he pulled against her, still screaming, clearly wanting *out* of the bed and not in.

"What's the matter?" Dillon's voice cut through the darkness beyond the flashlight's beam.

Darian heard it and ran to him, arms raised.

Dillon lifted him up and held him close as the screams continued. "Easy, dude," he said soothingly, patting Darian's back. "What's the problem? It is dark, but we're warm and safe. Look. Mom's right here."

Oh, God. Harper realized as her son's screams finally abated that Darian's problem had been Dillon's absence. In two brief days his little person had absorbed the comfort and sense of security Dillon provided, and he didn't want to be without it. Was it possible that the father and son bond had been forged that quickly?

Finally calm once again, Darian reached a little hand

out to Harper, sitting on the edge of the bed in her cotton nightgown. "Ma-ma!" he said urgently.

Dillon brought him back to her and tried to put him in her arms, but Darian held on fiercely and started screaming again.

He wanted both of them—and not on separate floors.

"All right, I get the message." Dillon reached a hand out to help Harper to her feet. "Let's give him what he wants before he wakes the twins and we don't get to sleep until Saturday. Grab the flashlight."

Darian was very happy when Dillon zipped two sleeping bags together and the three of them climbed into it.

Harper tried to keep a little distance from Dillon, knowing he'd created this intimacy simply for his son's sake. But the confines of the bag would not allow for distance, and she was finally forced to settle into Dillon's shoulder, their arms wrapped around Darian between them.

In minutes, the toddler was sound asleep.

"You read his mind," Harper said drowsily.

"All he wanted," Dillon replied, his voice flowing quietly over her in the darkness, "is life the way it should have been all along."

LIFE WENT ON with remarkable domesticity for four pleasant days. The babies were contented and responded to Harper and Dillon with lively appreciation of their attentions. Little limbs flailed and Cupid's-bow mouths moved into mysterious shapes. Gabrielle seldom fussed without reason, and Michelle, though more attuned to tension than was her sister, seemed to be relaxing into the routine.

Darian was fascinated by them and loved to sit with

Dillon and Harper when the babies were fed and played with. Harper was both pleased and distressed by the way he followed Dillon everywhere.

Harper and Dillon called his parents, and Harper explained about Darian. They sounded more excited than upset, though Harper was certain they must have felt somewhat betrayed, considering the friendship they'd maintained with her even while she was on the outs with their son.

"I'm so sorry," she said. "All I can say in my defense is that I didn't mean to hurt anyone. I was just doing what I thought was...best." That sounded so empty now.

"Don't be silly, Harper," Peg said, Charlie agreeing on a second phone. "Wouldn't we all like to take back the words and deeds that seemed right at the time and turned out not to be. We can't wait to meet him!"

Harper and Dillon bought sofas and chairs for the living room, and an extra crib for Darian, and a plumber arrived to install a john, a sink and a shower stall in a corner of the attic.

Bertie and Cliff took the babies and Darian for an afternoon while Harper helped Dillon wall off the little room. They threw a protective sheet over the dress form and the mirror, but didn't move them.

Harper was amazed that by dinnertime, they were ready to put up wallboard.

"That's a job for tomorrow," Dillon said as he and Harper admired their work. "You're not a bad carpenter's assistant."

"You're not a bad carpenter. I guess that comes from your brilliance in orthopedics."

"From my brilliance in general."

"Naturally."

They'd worked together like they used to in the old days, and teasing was suddenly easy and comfortable.

Dillon turned toward the middle of the room to get the full picture of Dori's bed and armoire in natural oak against the rough unfinished walls. The effect was rustic and charming.

"It needs a big, colorful rug," Harper suggested. "Something with red and gold. But I suppose it would only be fair to let Dori pick it out."

"Right." Then he indicated the covered dress form. "At some point, that's going to have to be moved out of the middle of the room."

"Dori doesn't mind it there," Harper said. "I don't think we should touch it—yet."

He frowned at her. "Are you afraid of upsetting Olivia?"

"No." Harper thought it through, knew it was crazy, but spoke her mind anyway in a slightly aggressive tone. "I'm afraid of upsetting what she's trying to do."

He looked skeptical. "You mean...arranging romance?"

"Skye seems to think that's her purpose."

"Come on," he chided.

"Okay." She shifted her weight. "I think I believe that, too. She helped Darrick and Skye fall in love. And she almost had us back together."

He said nothing, so she added intrepidly, "Maybe she's still working on us."

He met her gaze and held it. She couldn't tell whether that was something he wanted to think about or not.

"If that's the case," he said, heading for the stairs, "we'd better get out of here. She's going to need a lot of room to work."

DILLON WAS NAILING a picture hanger on the living room wall for the window frame Harper had decorated with moss and wildflowers when she ran through the room with a squeal and tore open the front door.

Skye and Dori burst in, also squealing. He turned with a fond shake of his head to watch a round of hugs exchanged, and to listen to high-pitched greetings that would have been impossible to separate into coherent words.

It was interesting to observe what happened when women liked each other, he thought. The noise level grew high and loud, and while the words weren't often decipherable, so much was expressed with eyes and touch. All in all, not a bad way to communicate.

He hung the window frame while they chattered; then, satisfied that it was well placed, he wandered toward their noisy little knot.

The moment he was noticed, *he* became the object of squeals, greetings and all the eye and touch action. Skye hugged him. Then Dori wrapped her arms around him, following the affectionate gesture with a slug to his arm—something she'd been doing since she was eight.

Then the three women moved in a wave to the red sofa where the twins were propped against a pillow, watching them with wide eyes. It was only a matter of time, he realized, until the twins became one of their number. They were girls, too—it was their rightful heritage.

"Mom and Dad and Darrick won't believe how much the angel babies have grown." Dori picked up one baby while Skye cuddled the other. Dori smiled tentatively at Dillon. "I'm supposed to warn you that we're all converging here on Sunday. Father's Day, you know.''

Dillon turned to Harper with a grim expression. ''Uh, oh. We need a card and a gift.''

''That'll be easy,'' she assured him, then turned to his sister. ''Dori, wait until you see your room!''

She looked hopeful. ''You mean it has furniture?''

''And a bathroom!''

''You're kidding!''

The squealing started all over again, and Dillon claimed the babies while the women paraded upstairs to scale the ladder and see for themselves.

Skye was the first one down. ''Can we steal Harper, take her to lunch and spend a couple of hours shopping? I have to drive back tonight and she and I have to compare new discoveries on Olivia.''

''Of course.'' He pulled a jar of peanut butter down from the cupboard and held it up, assuming a dramatic air of abuse. ''Why should I mind being left with two grumpy babies and a wild toddler while the three of you are out eating exotic things and having fun.''

She made a scornful sound and went to the refrigerator. ''Put the peanut butter away,'' she said without sympathy. ''I happen to have it on good authority that in this fridge is the best pasta salad known to man— or at least to Harper. And cold chicken breasts.'' She pulled out a covered bowl, closed the door and held out her hand. ''Fork, please.''

Dillon handed her one.

''Harper says you've been feeding her like royalty,'' she went on, dipping her fork into the cold, seasoned pasta, ''and that you have enough leftovers to see you through lunch. Oh. Oh!'' She rolled her eyes heavenward as she chewed and swallowed. She re-covered the bowl and replaced it. "But don't eat it all, because I'll need something to keep me going on the drive home."

He took the fork from her and tossed it into the sink. "So you're telling me that I can expect no more sympathy from you than I generally get from your husband?"

She laughed and went to the table where the babies lay in their carrier, asleep. She put a hand to each of them, her expression growing wistful.

Dillon remembered with a wrenching pain how she'd wept when she and Darrick had had to leave them.

But she drew a breath and seemed to toss off the emotion as she took a chair. "Actually, Darrick talks of you with great fondness and respect. It just seems important to him that you not know that he does. Something about keeping the kid brother in line."

He sat opposite her. "I can't tell you what I'd give to come back in another life as *his* older brother. And Duncan's, come to think of it. But maybe I should be telling this to Olivia."

Skye cupped her chin in her hand. "Maybe you should. She's just working one miracle after another."

"Skye," Dillon said patiently, "*God* works miracles. Ghosts just work mischief."

"Not so," she insisted. "Darrick and I...you and Harper..."

He debated whether or not to mention that a change had taken place there, when her sudden distraction from the conversation made it unnecessary.

Her eyes widened and her brow furrowed. "Who's that?" she demanded, pointing beyond him.

Dillon turned to see Darian wandering toward him, the bear in his arms. He was just getting up from a nap in the downstairs bedroom.

Dillon pulled the boy into his lap. "This," he said with a "brace yourself" glance at her, "is your nephew—my son, Darian."

Smiling, but obviously shocked, she came to kneel beside him as Darian clung to him, eyeing her interestedly. "He's yours...too?"

"Yes."

"But...Darrick doesn't know." She looked confused. "Does he?"

"No. I just found out myself less than a week ago. We just got through to Mom and Dad, and I was going to call you, but here you are."

She studied Darian a little more closely, then put a fingertip to his little nose. He giggled. "I see Harper in that little face, don't I?"

He nodded. "That you do."

"But why...?"

"It's complicated. She thought she had her reasons for keeping him a secret."

Dori came down the stairs, and this time Harper, who accompanied her, had to explain.

"Do Mom and Dad know?" Dori asked.

Dillon nodded. "Under duress, Mom agreed to leave the spreading of the news to us. I intended to get to it in the next few days."

Dori leaned over Darian, and he smiled but hid his face in Dillon's shirt.

"Well," she observed, straightening. "It didn't take you two long to hit it off."

Harper rolled her eyes. "Don't get me started. I'm his mother for fifteen months and he abandons me for his father the day they meet. Men!"

Dillon gave her a look that was only half-teasing. "Sort of serves you right, doesn't it?"

She made a face at him. "I may or may not be home for dinner."

DILLON AND DARIAN WALKED the women out to Skye's car.

"You're sure you'll be all right?" Harper asked as he opened the back door for her.

"I'll be fine," he said for the fourth time. "But you could bring me back something to comfort me just in case."

"Okay, what?"

"I don't know. Whatever appeals to you."

"Edible? Wearable?"

He grinned just as she caught the drift of his thought.

Skye put it into words. "Something that's wearable for you and edible for him could clear away the stress of somebody's fibbing nature."

"Skye McKeon!" she grumbled. "*You* should talk."

"Takes one to know one," she retorted with no apparent regret.

Harper climbed into the car.

Dillon leaned down to look into the front across Dori to Skye. "Drive carefully," he warned. "Remember that you're driving a car and not flying a plane."

Skye waved, then backed out of the driveway with a squeal of tires and drove off in a roar. All three waved at him, laughing.

He rolled his eyes heavenward and wondered if it broke protocol for a Presbyterian to invoke St. Christopher.

HARPER, SKYE AND DORI stood in a small half circle, staring up at the carpet that hung from the ceiling in the Dancer's Beach Department Store's housewares department. It was a deep red patterned with triangular stylized green trees and yellow moons. Interspersed here and there were small brown moose.

"That's it!" Dori said, then turned to her companions. "What do you think?"

"Perfect!" Skye agreed.

Harper nodded, visualizing the carpet laid out before the dress form and the mirror. "Yes!"

They carried it back to the car, then went in search of a Father's Day gift for Charlie. They started in Used But Enthused.

Harper didn't find what she was looking for, but Skye pointed to the wall and cried delightedly, "Guys, look!"

Harper and Dori turned in unison. Hanging above the cash register was a worn wooden sign with a golfer wearing argyles painted on it. It read, Duffers Crossing.

All three started laughing.

"Is that perfect for Darrick?" Skye began digging into her purse.

Once they'd purchased the sign, had it wrapped and carried it back to the car, they moved on to a men's shop. Dori bought a robe with a crown crest on the pocket, and Harper was undecided between a gray cotton sweater and a natty, broad-brimmed straw hat.

"I vote for the hat," Skye said.

Harper nodded. "I like it, too, but would he wear it?"

"If you gave it to him." Dori made a face at her. "He thinks you're wonderful. I think he likes you better than me."

"Well, who wouldn't," Harper said seriously, then broke into laughter when Dori gasped indignantly.

"Someone who might have liked to know he had a son," Dori replied pointedly.

Harper nodded, prepared to take the heat. "You're right. He's pretty upset with me. I know I was wrong, but at the time..." She shook her head, unable to explain herself now that she looked back on it. She sighed. "I don't know. Can I claim insanity?"

Dori put an arm around her shoulders. "If that'd work for anyone, it'd work for you." At Harper's feigned hurt feelings, she added, "Oh, buck up. I owed you that one."

"You buy the hat," Skye finally said when conversation was back on track again, "and I'll buy the sweater on the chance that Darrick hasn't thought about a Father's Day gift. If he has, we'll just save it for Christmas."

"Very practical," Dori praised. "Darrick would be proud of you. That's scary, you know. I try never to do anything Darrick would be proud of."

Laughing, they made their way to the counter.

Packages stored away again, they bought iced mochas to go, and took them to the little park half a block away. It was protected from the street by a border of old ash trees. Children laughed and called to one another on the playground on the far side of the park, but the other side was still and quiet, picnic tables unoccupied, afternoon sun dappling one particular one through the protective trees.

Harper headed for it, anxious to sit and rest her feet. "I haven't shopped like this since Christmas!"

Skye and Dori sat across the table from her, both groaning as they climbed in between the table and the bench.

"That has to be a fib. You must have been shopping

day and night.'' Skye said, then paused to take a long
sip of her drink. ''That is *so* good,'' she said in an
aside, then continued, ''Because the house is full of
new furniture, and also full of all that great old stuff
you and Dillon have refinished.''

''No, just a couple of after—'' Harper stopped
abruptly when some extra sense warned her of danger.
She noticed that Skye's expression had changed also,
and that she was staring at something behind Harper.

Dori, staring in the same direction, put a hand to her
eyes and muttered grimly, ''Oh, no.''

Harper turned and saw three men coming toward
them from the trees. They appeared to be Latino, and
were informally but elegantly dressed—all in black.
They walked wide apart, as though their intention was
to prevent either her or one of her companions from
escaping.

Her brain, trying to make sense of the weird data,
cast aside the oddities of the situation and processed it
simply as trouble. That decision reached, she swung
her legs over the bench and sprang to her feet, mentally
reviewing what she'd learned in karate class. She leapt
at the man who appeared to be the vanguard of the
small attack force.

She heard Dori's shout—''Harper! No!''—but she
was concentrating on taking the man down. She'd been
an ''adopted'' McKeon long enough to hold Dori and
Skye as dear as sisters.

She swung and jabbed at the tall Latino, who countered her moves by simply stopping her rather than
striking back. When she squared off with him and
found him smiling, hands up as he prepared to block
her next move, her brain began to reassess the situation.
The smile wasn't scornful or predatory. It was the same

smile Dillon gave her when she did something that surprised him and he wasn't sure how to react.

Then Dori and Skye were flanking her, holding her back. "It's all right," Dori said urgently, frowning at the man. "I know them. They're not here to hurt us."

Harper drew a deep breath and tried to appraise the new information. "Then, who are they? Why are they here?"

"I can answer that," Skye said, holding Harper's other arm. "This is Señor Salvatore Dominguez, and I believe he's here to annoy Dori."

The man, absolutely gorgeous at closer inspection, wore a black silk T-shirt and black slacks. He inclined his head gallantly.

"Mr. Dominguez," Skye continued, "this is Harper Harriman, my brother-in-law's friend."

Dominguez had a devastating smile. "Mrs. McKeon," he said to Skye with another bow, then to Harper, "I hope your friend knows how to defend himself."

"I told you I would be in touch." Dori stepped between her companions and Dominguez. "You have no right to follow me around."

"I have every right," he corrected her. His manner changing subtly, Harper noticed, his good manners in place, but his tone edgy. With Dori, it seemed he was protecting himself from more than physical attack. "But let us not waste time over something that is of no importance." He smiled at the other two women. "Please sit down. We'll only be a moment."

He said something in Spanish to the two men who accompanied him, and they took positions, one on either side of the table. Harper couldn't decide if their presence was intended to prevent her and Skye from leaving, or to prevent someone else from getting to them.

Then he took Dori's arm and led her a small distance away.

"What is going on?" Harper demanded of Skye in a whisper.

"I'm not sure." Skye sipped at her drink and frowned at the spot where Dominguez had Dori backed up against a tree, leaving a small distance between them.

"It has something to do with a friend of Dori's named Julietta. This man represents Julietta's father, who, if I haven't dreamed all this, is a cat burglar, or something."

"What?"

"I know. It's all very bizarre. But it seems this Julietta and her father had a major quarrel about what he does for a living, just before her father and his gang were surprised by police in the middle of a…job. Or does one call them heists?"

Harper made a face at Skye. "I don't know. My cat burgling vocabulary is limited. They were all caught?"

"No, they all escaped, but Julietta's father broke his arm and his gang dispersed. They've all been hiding out ever since."

"But why is this guy here to ask *Dori* about Julietta?"

"Because Julietta's in hiding also. Not only are the police looking for her to make her tell them where her father is, but while she's hiding, she's also trying to find out who really did rat on them—not an easy task. Dori seems to think everyone involved is in danger until Julietta finds out who it is."

"You're kidding! And Dori knows where she is?"

"Dori's hiding her."

"God. Where? Who is she?"

Skye picked up her mocha. "I don't know. I thought she might be you."

"What?" Harper stared in wide-eyed astonishment. "Why?"

Skye sipped from her cup, then put it down and looked her in the eye. "Because whoever she is, she's the real mother of the twins."

"Oh, my God." Harper struggled to absorb that, to consider the ramifications. "Our...twins?" she asked, hoping she'd misunderstood.

"Our twins."

"Then it must be...Allison Cartier." Harper thought about it. "She's always halfway across the world, and she's been out of sight for months. It fits, Skye!"

Skye frowned over that, playing with the straw in her empty cup. "I don't know. I suppose it's possible. But wouldn't someone at the hospital in Edenfield have recognized her when she went there to have the twins?"

Harper was considering that when Dori and Dominguez came back to the table.

"Ladies, I apologize again for alarming you," Dominguez said, looking from one to the other. "We'll be on our way." He focused on Dori. "Please see that you are punctual for our next meeting."

"Goodbye, Sal," Dori said firmly.

He smiled at her. "Until we meet again."

"Good*bye!*"

He blew her a kiss and walked away, his companions falling into step behind him.

Dori leaned her elbows on the table and covered her face with her hands.

"Okay, I want the entire story," Harper said, taking one of Dori's hands and lowering it to the table so that Dori was forced to look at her. "And I want it right now. To think *you* were scolding *me* for keeping secrets! If your brothers or your parents had any idea what you're doing, they'd—"

Dori turned to Harper, her delicate jaw set in firm lines. "They'd have a fit, I know. That's why you're not going to say a word."

"Dori…!"

"Harper." Dori took hold of her arms and gave her a shake. "Listen to me. My friend has two little babies she can't even be with because the police are after her and she has to stay in hiding to protect them and her father. Please don't make things any harder for her."

"But if *you're* in danger, Dillon—the family would want to know!"

"Absolutely not! They'd step into the middle, determined to solve it all for me, and bring Julie out, which would reveal her to the police and put her in the position of having to testify against her father."

Harper suddenly related very closely to the unknown Julietta's predicament. Something very important just occurred to her. "So, if this Julie is your friend, and you're hiding her, then she must have told you which brother fathered the twins."

Dori shook her head and sighed heavily. "No, she didn't. She figures if no one knows who the real father is, then we're all safer."

Harper looked doubtfully at Skye. "Does that make sense to you?"

Skye shook her head. "No, but I'm just trying to believe that she knows what she's doing. And when it comes to the crunch, the guys are all smart enough to save themselves and each other, so until we do know what's going on, maybe it's safer just to coast.''

Harper's eyes widened in disbelief. ''While Dori's dealing on the side with a crime family?''

''They're not a crime family,'' Dori said in a sort of reluctant defense. ''They're just a family that's into theft. It's not the same thing. And in their favor, they use the money they make to support a couple of poor little villages in Mexico that nobody cares about.''

Harper gasped as the story grew more and more unbelievable. ''You mean like Robin Hood, Mexican-style?''

Skye nodded and smiled. ''I like to think of them as Zorros.''

Harper shook her head in bewilderment, then finished her mocha, hoping the caffeine would help clear her brain. It did somewhat, but a clear picture of the situation was not necessarily comforting.

''How did Julie's family find you?'' she asked Dori.

''They didn't,'' Dori replied. ''I found them. I helped Julie hide right after New Orleans, then went on to Oxford. When I came home, Julie asked me to find her father and tell him that she was all right, and that she wasn't the one who'd sold them out to the police.''

''What do you mean, that she was all right?''

''She was out of touch with them for a couple of months right after the failed job. She had to be out of reach of the police, but she had to support herself, so I found her a job out of the country. She came home to have the babies, but when her father showed up at the hospital, she took off because she knew the police were right behind her, too, and she didn't want them to find him.''

"What a mess!"

"You can say that again."

"And you can't tell us who she is."

"No."

"And you can't tell us *where* she is."

"That's right."

"And you can't tell us which of your brothers is the father."

"Because I don't know."

"And you expect Skye and me to keep this all secret?!"

Dori put an arm around Skye's shoulders. "Skye's been doing it since she flew me to Seattle a month ago to meet Julietta's father."

Harper looked at Skye in frowning disapproval.

Skye raised a placating hand. "I didn't know that was what I was doing at the time. But now that it's done, and now that you're involved, I don't see why we can't just work this out ourselves. Let's just do what it takes to keep the McKeons safe."

Harper looked from one to the other and knew that despite all her reservations about the wisdom of this course of action, they were bound together by love for the McKeons.

"All right," she said, climbing off the bench. "But it's going to take a really *big* dessert to buy my silence."

Chapter Ten

Harper and Dillon, with the twins in their arms, and Darian holding Dillon's hand, stood in the driveway as Skye slipped in behind the wheel of her car. Dori handed her a brown-paper bag of snacks Dillon had packed to sustain Skye on the drive home.

"If everyone's going to be here Sunday," Dillon said to Skye, "I don't see why you didn't just arrange to stay with us."

"I have something to do tomorrow," she said with a mysterious smile. "Darrick and I'll have a surprise for you on Sunday."

"What is it?" Harper asked.

Skye turned the key in the ignition. "A surprise means I don't tell you what it is until you're surprised!" she said over the sound of the motor. She blew them all a kiss. "See you Sunday. Love you! Take care of our babies!"

Dillon watched her drive away, a thoughtful expression on his face.

"You like her?" Dori asked.

He nodded. "A lot. I can't believe Darrick was smart enough to find her. I wonder what kind of wife Duncan will bring home one day."

"Probably some gorgeous thing with perfect makeup," she grumbled, "and panty hose-advertisement legs. I'll have to kill her." She caught Darian's other hand and they all turned toward the house. "I don't suppose I have to remind you that *you* haven't officially brought home a wife yet?"

"No, you don't," he said, turning to look at Harper, who followed them inside. "I'm working on it."

"I'm just warning you that I expect to be in the wedding," Dori said, taking Gabrielle from him. "I was in Darrick's, you know."

"Yes, while I was away stamping out disease."

"Well, that's what you get for gallivanting. You wouldn't miss so much if you stayed around more."

Dillon studied Harper with mild accusation in the tilt of his eyebrow. "You bribed her to say that."

"I did not," Harper denied.

"I came to that conclusion myself." Gabrielle smiled at Dori and she smiled back, leaning closer to nuzzle the baby. Then she leveled a friendly but judicious gaze on her brother. "Life's getting pretty thick in this family. Wives, babies, roots. Your work is noble, but if you don't want to miss your *whole* life, you may have to slow down enough to live it."

"Well, tell the world to stop having health crises."

"Well, tell yourself you're not the only one who can handle them."

With that, Dori walked away, calling over her shoulder, "I'm going to make some iced tea. Anybody want some?"

"Please," Harper replied. "You?" she asked Dillon.

He looked mildly disgruntled. "Take mine and pour it over my little sister. I'm going into the garage to work on the old loveseat."

HARPER SAT IN THE MIDDLE of the new carpet, the fabric Bertie had given her in her lap. She took tiny stitches in it, looking up occasionally to watch Dori, who lay across her bed. The twins were asleep on the coverlet beside her, and Darian had joined his father in the garage.

"Speaking of life becoming thick," Harper said, "tell me about Salvatore Dominguez. Did I detect something there?"

Dori frowned at her, chin propped in the palm of her hand. "Like what?"

"Like attraction?"

Dori made a scornful sound. "Maybe on *his* part."

"That's what I meant."

Dori lowered her hands and leaned on her forearms. "Did you? Did you think he seemed...interested?"

Harper was surprised by Dori's hopeful look. "Yes. Are you interested?"

"He's a thief."

"But that's not what I asked you."

Dori sat up and settled herself cross-legged, leaning over to resettle the light blanket over the babies. Then she made a face, intended, Harper guessed, to convey confusion. "He's...strangely appealing," she said finally, "but he's bossy and arrogant. And, at the risk of being repetitious, he's a thief. I could never be serious about someone like that."

Harper nodded. That sounded sensible. Still, there was something in the way Dominguez looked at Dori that made Harper think he just might change his world for her.

"How does he happen to be with your friend's father?"

Dori made a hands-up, helpless gesture. "I don't

know a thing about him. When I tried to reach Julie's father, he's the one who got in touch with me.''

"Maybe when this is over," Harper suggested, "you and he can...you know...see if there's anything valid between you.''

"Her father will have to give himself up for it to be over, and I don't think he'll do that because then the little villages he supports will starve.''

"Well, she can't be separated from her babies and her father for the rest of her life," Harper insisted. "There has to be a solution.''

Dori nodded. "One would hope so. But right now, I can't see what it is.''

"We'll find one." Harper readjusted her mound of fabric. "Skye's a good ally. We'll come up with something.''

Dori's friend *had* to be Allison. Harper just knew it. While it was true that no one at the hospital had recognized her, as a photographer Harper knew all too well that a woman made up for television could look very different without makeup. Or she might have deliberately *tried* to appear incognito. Harper wondered if Dillon had any idea about Allison's family.

"What about solutions for you?" Dori asked, easing herself off the bed carefully so as not to wake the twins. "Are you going to marry Dillon?''

"He hasn't asked me," Harper evaded.

"Come on. He's always loved you. You're the one who stopped loving *him* because of his work with the medical team. And, my God! You two have Darian!''

"I stopped," Harper corrected, concentrating on her tiny stitches, "because he refused to work with me. Even when our wedding was only a month away, I couldn't get him interested in talking about the future.

You said it yourself earlier. He's savior to the world, but he's missing his own life. That's why I didn't tell him about his son. First, because I couldn't even reach him, and then because I knew he couldn't be there for Darian any more than he could for me.''

''But Dillon isn't missing anything right now.''

Harper gave Dori a wry glance. ''That's because the world hasn't called him to a crisis in the past few weeks. We'll see what happens when it does.''

There was silence for a moment while Dori sighed, probably accepting that that could be true.

''What are you making, anyway?'' Dori asked finally. ''And where'd you get that fabric?''

Harper told her about the gift from Bertie. ''I thought I'd make a skirt to go with Olivia's bodice. I started working on it a couple of days ago.'' She stood, shook out the fabric and held it up for Dori's inspection. It was the popular gored skirt of the period, but she had yet to hem it and make a waistband. ''What do you think?''

''I think it'll be beautiful.'' Dori had pulled the protective sheet off the dress form when she took up residence, and now she stood beside it, encouraging Harper to hold the skirt up to the bodice. ''Bring it here. Let's see how it looks.''

Harper complied. ''I made the waistband dip to a point in the front so that it sort of matches the beading.''

''It's too bad it's too late for Olivia to wear it,'' Dori said sadly.

Harper smiled. ''Well, maybe it'll be in time for you to wear it.''

Dori made a face at her. ''I'm not getting married.''

''You will one day.'' Harper held the skirt up to

Dori. "It's Skye's theory that this bodice was intended to help us all find our loves. And you're Olivia's size. Skye's too tall and I'm too short. It'd make the perfect wedding dress for you."

Dori held the skirt to herself and studied her reflection in the mirror. Then she turned the dress form to face it and stood behind it, standing on tiptoe to place her body so that her face and throat appeared just above Olivia's handiwork.

The fit *would* be perfect. Harper felt a punch to her ribs. *Was* the bodice meant for Dori?

Dori admired her reflection for a moment, then with a sigh of disgust handed Harper the skirt and put the dress form back where it had been. "This is ridiculous. *We're* ridiculous. I'm going to get some work done on my thesis while the girls are sleeping."

"I'll get out of your hair," Harper said, gathering up her things. "I should do an inventory check for groceries for the weekend."

"Please lay in some chocolate. I'm going to need it."

WHEN DILLON'S FAMILY burst into his life on special occasions and holidays, he always felt as though someone had turned up the planet's volume. That sensation was enhanced on Father's Day afternoon when his parents arrived in a camper with a puppy, and Darrick and Skye arrived right behind them with a son.

His father carried in a golden retriever that Dillon guessed to be about three months old. Its russet hair was already luxurious, big dark eyes bright and winning.

His mother followed with two blue plastic food bowls, a red leash and a bag of puppy food.

"Ah…" Dillon began, stepping back to allow them entrance.

They trooped in like an ad for the pet department of the local supermarket. His mother smiled at him. "Relax. It's not for you, it's for David."

"Who's David?" he asked.

"That's me!" a loud raspy voice said.

Dillon turned to see who'd spoken and found himself staring at Darrick and Skye.

Darrick pointed down.

Dillon lowered his gaze and looked into the upturned freckled face of a boy about five or six. He was sturdily built, had a sandy-colored buzz cut and wire-rimmed glasses.

"Hi." Completely surprised, Dillon offered his hand. "I'm Dillon."

The boy shook his hand. "You're my uncle," he informed him.

"I am?" Dillon swung his confused glance to Darrick.

"It's in the works," Darrick said, putting a hand to the boy's shoulder. "I'll explain it all later. I'd have called to warn you, but Skye thought it'd be fun to surprise you."

Dillon framed the boy's face in his hands and looked down at him. All surprises should look so hopeful and bright, he thought. "I am. But I'm also very happy. I've never been an uncle before," he said to the boy. "This'll be cool."

"I had one," David told him matter-of-factly, "but he died with my mom and my dad. And my aunt, too. They were on a plane."

For an instant, Dillon didn't know what to say.

David saved him by turning to Dillon's parents, who

looked as horrified as Dillon felt. He pointed to the wriggling puppy. "Is he really for me?" David asked.

"These are your grandparents," Skye said. "Grandma Peg and Grandpa Charlie."

Big tears slid down Peg's cheeks as she handed him the puppy, then leaned down to hug him.

David looked at her in concern.

"Don't worry about her," Charlie said, taking the boy into his arms. "She cries all the time when she's happy. And she's really happy you're going to be part of the family."

"Me, too," David said, then dissolved into giggles when the puppy licked his face. "What's his name?"

"We thought *you'd* like to give him a name," Charlie said.

After less than five seconds' thought, David decided. "Hercules!"

When Charlie raised an eyebrow at the child's knowledge of mythology, Skye explained with a grin, "We saw the Disney movie last weekend."

"We have a surprise, too," Harper said, appearing beside Dillon with Darian in her arms. "David, this is your cousin Darian. Everybody, your nephew, your grandson."

"I've heard about you." Darrick held out his hands and Darian looked him over, then decided he looked enough like Dillon to be trusted and went to him.

"Why don't we take Hercules into the backyard," Skye suggested, "so he doesn't piddle in the house. He's probably pretty excited."

The family wandered through the house and out to the backyard.

"Guess I'll have to wait my turn with Darian," Charlie said. "Beautiful boy, son."

"Thanks, Dad. He's a character. Smart, nosy, loving."

"That's probably because *he's* been loved. You trying to see her side of this?"

"Don't nag, Dad. I'm working on it."

Charlie diplomatically changed the subject to David, beckoning Dillon outside with him to the motor home. "One of the nuns who counsels at the hospital knew David was in foster care, and when Darrick mentioned to her that he and Skye wanted to adopt, she got the wheels in motion a little faster than they expected." He opened the back door of the motor home and smiled happily. "So in the space of less than two months, your mother and I have gone from no grandchildren to four. I'd like to see Bill and Sandra Wentworth match that efficiency."

Dillon knew the Wentworths were a couple in his parents' poker club. Peg and Charlie claimed the Wentworths were always touting their children's accomplishments, but that their children had produced no grandchildren. His mother loved having the edge in that department—the only one that counted, she claimed.

"And a camper!" Dillon noted. "When'd you get this?"

"Just picked it up used," his father replied. "Since we're always hauling stuff around to you kids, we thought we might as well have something to do it in without having to rent a little trailer. This is comfortable, too."

Charlie reached into the back and handed Dillon a large box. Pictured on it was a pirate ship and several small eye-patched figures. That was followed by the castle version of the same toy complete with knights and ladies and armored horses.

"How come I never had one of those?" Dillon complained.

His father handed out several children's books which he stacked on top of the pile in Darrick's arms. "Because we never really liked you, so we gave all the good stuff to your brothers."

"Then how come you keep visiting me?"

Charlie put a cowboy hat on Dillon's head. "Because we like the way you cook. Can you carry that inside and come back for the easel?"

THEY SAT IN THE BACKYARD as sunset turned to twilight, and drank coffee laced with brandy. They'd barbecued chicken and corn for dinner and rounded out the meal with Dillon's pasta salad, a potato salad and a fruit salad.

Everyone had gone in for jackets and sweaters against the evening cool, but sat back again comfortably unwilling to abandon the fragrant glow of evening.

Charlie was surrounded by gifts and wrapping, and jauntily wore the straw hat Harper had picked out for him.

Skye had given Darrick the Duffers Crossing sign, and the senior McKeons had brought each of their sons two padded lawn chairs "for sitting with the children and talking over the facts of life." They'd been immediately pressed into service—for the sitting, anyway.

The afternoon Harper had shopped with Skye and Dori, she'd bought Dillon a nubby oatmeal-colored sweater that was perfect for the cool coastal evening. She'd had Darian give it to him and he'd seemed touched, his eyes finding hers across the crowd. She thought she recognized some of the old heat in them. He'd pulled it on right over his shirt.

Darian had reclaimed the box and was now collecting napkins and plastic utensils to put in it.

Harper hadn't mentioned the episode in the park because she'd promised Dori that she wouldn't, but she often thought about it with concern.

Tonight, though, it was hard to worry about anything. Peg and Charlie each held one of the babies, securely wrapped against the cool evening.

Skye and Darrick sat side by side on a blanket on the grass and watched David playing with the puppy, love clear on their faces.

Dori sat on a lawn chair, looking up at the sky. Harper thought she knew who she was thinking about, judging by the look on her face: a combination of dreaminess and consternation.

Harper and Dillon sat side by side in lawn chairs. She did her best to keep breathing when he put an arm around her shoulders.

"Thank you for the sweater," he said, his lips at her ear to be heard over the family's cheerful tumult.

"You're welcome." She turned to look into his eyes, a little surprised by the gentleness there. "You're a wonderful father." She felt choked and emotional. "And now you're an uncle as well."

He smiled. "My life's taken some amazing leaps."

That was true, and *he'd* taken those leaps all with remarkable grace. But how was she going to fit into the rest of his life? Was that what he was suggesting he wanted?

Unable to decide for certain, she went back to the safer subject of his new nephew. "David's the cutest thing," she whispered back. "And that voice. He sounds like Louis Armstrong might have before his voice changed."

Dillon laughed.

"Remember," Peg said, her voice just a little fragile, "when Donovan brought home that St. Bernard?"

Harper felt the smallest reaction in Dillon. This often happened when the family got together. The subject of Donovan inevitably arose, not because the McKeons weren't complete as they were, but because Donovan had once belonged and would always belong—even though memories of him were painful.

"Yeah." Darrick didn't take his eyes off David. "He said he found it."

"He did," Dillon said, a small smile forming. "He found it in the Fergusons' backyard in their dog run."

"He didn't like to see things confined," Charlie said, hugging Peg to him with his free arm. "He'd been confined so much himself since he was diagnosed."

David looked up from petting the puppy, who'd finally collapsed against him in a furry golden heap. "I know about Donovan," he said gravely.

Harper felt Dillon's arm tense around her.

"You do?" Peg asked, her voice tremulous.

David nodded. "Darrick told me. He died."

There was a moment's silence as a fragrant breeze wafted through their company, and surf riffled in the distance on the other side of the road.

"Darrick says my mom and dad are probably taking care of him for you now," David continued, "like Darrick and Skye are taking care of me. It's like God did a swap." He turned to Darrick for corroboration. "Right?"

Darrick took a moment to clear his throat. "Right."

Peg put a hand to her mouth, and David went to her. She'd been sneaking him and Darian sweet treats all afternoon, and a relationship was already underway. He put his arm around her shoulder and patted it. She hugged him to her fiercely. "It's supposed to be this way 'cause I'm a D, too. Like Darrick and Dillon and Donovan and Darian and...who's the other one?"

"Duncan," Darrick provided.

"You forgot Dori," Dori pointed out, pretending hurt feelings.

"But you're a girl," he said with a laugh.

"You mean girls don't count?" she demanded.

David turned to Darrick.

Darrick shook his head. "That's a trick question, Dave. Don't answer it."

The women all frowned at one another.

"Maybe we should just leave," Skye suggested. "We're clearly not appreciated."

David went to sit in her lap. "No. I want you to stay."

"But you said girls don't count."

"But you guys aren't girls. You're a mom and a grandma and my aunts. I like you."

"Moms and aunts and grandmas are girls."

David thought that over. Then he turned to Darrick, whom he seemed to think had the answers to everything. "So, we like girls, right?"

"Yeah, pretty much. They couldn't get along very well without us, so we let them hang around."

Skye and Dori pinned Darrick to the blanket and pummeled him. David went to his defense, giggling uproariously.

Peg's tears and Dillon's tension turned to laughter.

"I CAN'T BELIEVE we have beds to sleep in," Darrick said as he and Skye prepared to climb the stairs. Peg and Charlie had already retired, and Dori had climbed into her attic room.

Dillon indicated the sleeping boy in Darrick's arms. "One of the sofas is a sleeper. You want to leave him down here?"

Darrick shook his head. "No, he was excited about getting to sleep in a sleeping bag. He'll be fine."

Dillon smiled. "He's a great kid."

Skye stroked the head lolling on Darrick's shoulder. "Yeah, we think so, too." Then she indicated the twins asleep in the carrier on the kitchen table. "I can't believe how big they're getting. Pretty soon they won't fit in there together anymore."

"I know." Dillon rolled his eyes. "Then we get to tote *two* carriers everywhere. *And* chase Darian."

"You hear from Allison What's-her-name?" Darrick asked.

"No, nothing yet. She's still somewhere in Palestine."

"So the mystery continues."

"For the moment."

"Okay. Anything you need us to do before we go up?"

"Not a thing. Dishwasher's going, Dad's gifts are in the motor home. I think all's well."

"All right. Good night."

Harper watched a little jealously as the three went upstairs.

"What's that greedy gleam for?" Dillon asked her as he took eggs and milk out of the refrigerator.

She sighed and went to lean against the counter, where he placed a bowl and a whisk. "I was just admiring Darrick and Skye's...their sort of..." She linked her fingers together, groping for the right word.

"Their security in each other," Dillon said for her, pulling the flour and sugar canisters toward him.

There was no condemnation in his eyes, she noticed, just a little of the same sadness she felt.

"We've never quite been able to find that in our relationship, have we?"

She thought about that, and realized how different she was now from the woman she'd been when Darian was conceived.

"No, but I don't think we're the same people we were then," she replied, watching as he cracked an egg on the side of the bowl and split it with one hand. "We might do a better job of being in love now."

He dropped the shell in the sink, wiped his hands on a towel and leaned against the counter facing her. He grinned. "You'd be happy with three babies under two?"

She'd be deliriously happy, she thought, but there was still the problem of the twins' mother.

The sad and complex details Dori had attached to the tale of her friend who'd had the babies might very well apply to Allison—but Dillon didn't know that and Harper had promised not to tell. She wanted to believe things would work out the way he insisted they would, but she knew that when he found out the truth about why the babies were left, he might feel differently.

So the present was all she had.

"Would you be happy?" For days she'd been afraid to take the liberty of touching him, but she did so now, looping her arms around his neck, luxuriating in the feel of him once again.

Dillon wrapped his arms around her and pulled her close. "I would be very happy."

"I'm sorry about Darian," she whispered, tears in her throat.

He tightened his grip on her. "I know. I understand. Let's concentrate now on what lies ahead of us. Now, go warm up the bed so I can get this in the refrigerator. I'll meet you upstairs."

THEY MADE LOVE FOR HOURS—passion and tenderness, tension and exuberance all woven together to give their communication a depth and texture that was both satisfying and mystifying.

Were they finally learning to compromise? Harper wondered as she rose over him to take him inside her for the third time. He clasped hands with her as he filled her, and she thought, with the onset of a dizzying and delicious torment as he moved beneath her, that sensation seemed to brim beyond her ability to contain it.

She uttered a little gasp, feeling as though she had to hurry to keep pace with it, to work harder not to lose a moment.

Then Dillon wrapped his arms around her thighs and held. "I know," he said softly. "Just let it happen. You don't have to chase it or contain it or analyze it. Just let it be what it is. Slow down."

But the tightening spiral of sensation was an urgent thing.

He moved again and climax hit her like a comet, streaks of fire raining over and inside her.

He linked his hands with hers to steady her as she arched backward.

Her mind spun, sensation rolling over everything—thought, comprehension, ability to speak.

Dillon took great pleasure and satisfaction in her little frenzied cries. He'd wanted her to lose control completely, to remember how good they were together, to forget all the possible obstacles to their future together and to remember only that it had to be.

She said his name with desperation as though a door were closing between them, then her body tightened around him.

He lost awareness of everything but the pulse of the love that flowed through him into her. It was powerful stuff—star fuel—and he felt it fill his being even as he filled her.

She collapsed on him, breathing heavily, and lay there for long moments. Then she pushed against his shoulders and looked down at him, her eyes reflecting the moonlight from the window.

"What have you been doing?" she demanded playfully.

He pretended confusion. "You mean you didn't notice?"

She swatted his ribs. "I mean, have you been working out? Taking vitamins?"

"Nah." He laughed lightly. "In fact, I've been raising babies and missing sleep. You're the power source. When it's right, it's right."

She lay down on him again, kissed his throat, then nuzzled into his shoulder with a deep sigh. "It's so right that even if it was wrong, it'd be right."

Sometimes, Dillon mused, her thought processes were too complicated for him. But it was easy to agree on the perfection of their union. "Yes," he whispered.

Chapter Eleven

Dillon remembered clearly what it had been like to have three brothers and no sister. When he was five, Donovan had been alive, and Dori hadn't been born yet. The McKeons had been a strong, cohesive unit.

He recalled as though he'd experienced it yesterday how it had felt to be the youngest. His brothers had picked on him, blamed him, tricked him and suckered him. But he'd quickly learned that all he had to do was shriek and his mother or father would come running. Duncan or Darrick or Donovan would be interrogated and he would have time to escape.

But Duncan had always been there to offer calming advice, Darrick to organize the situation to make the bad parts of it go away and the good parts multiply, and Donovan to make him laugh. When he'd proven that he could take their persecution without shrieking for help, he'd finally been accepted into their gang. He thought of them as a gang because the concept of a "club" was simply too civilized for their brand of camaraderie.

Then Donovan was gone and there were just the three of them. It had been a difficult adjustment. Dillon had cried a lot, but the others hadn't teased him for it. He knew they'd cried, too.

Time wore on and as they grew older, he and Duncan and Darrick became more of a team than a gang. Dori was born, and they had a common purpose to protect her from anything that might hurt her—from bees to street traffic.

It was strange, he thought philosophically—sitting at the dining room table over a third cup of coffee and the rubble of breakfast—how their relationship continued to evolve.

In the living room, Harper had sat Darrick and Skye on the loveseat, draped a Manchester Linens sheet across both of them from his hip to her shoulder, and then given each of them one of the twins. She tucked David in next to Skye, then stepped back, her camera set up to immortalize the picture they made. Hercules leapt up into the middle, licking faces.

Dillon was surprised at the ease with which Darrick had taken on the role of husband and father. He'd always been the orderly one, the one who made sense of chaos and organized the impossible. And judging by what Dillon knew of love so far, it defied order and organization, and made you feel as though your life would *always* be chaos.

But then again, that described life in a relocation camp, or a field hospital, or an emergency shelter, so Dillon was no stranger to it.

But Darrick? Paradoxically, he seemed to be thriving.

Harper took several shots, then moved David in between Darrick and Skye, put the twins in his lap, and shot several more times.

Then she replaced them with Peg and Charlie.

"I thought their motto had to do with a 'nursery.'" His father complained good-naturedly as Harper draped his arm around his mother's shoulders. "We'll make it look like it involves a convalescent home."

"Or a casino," Darrick offered from the sidelines.

His mother cast him a frown. Harper put the babies in their laps and wrapped a blanket around all of them.

"But I'm hot," his father complained again.

Smiling at the camera, his mother said, "Charlie, you haven't been hot in thirty years."

Harper shot a picture of the frown he gave her as the entire room erupted into laughter.

Dillon swallowed a lump in his throat, surprised that it was there. Love never died, he realized. It simply metamorphosed to fit where it was needed, to close in and tighten the ranks when it had to—as when Donovan died, or when newcomers arrived, like the twins, and Skye, and David.

Harper had been around too long to be considered a newcomer. She was already family.

All he had to do was make it legal.

When Dori wandered through in shorts and a T-shirt after a walk on the beach, Harper replaced Dillon's parents with her, put both babies in her lap, and sat Darian beside her. The toddler, accustomed to being photographed, hammed. She threw a Manchester Linens towel over Dori's shoulder and shot right in the middle of Dori's startled, "What is going on?"

Harper explained while she took the towel from her shoulder and wrapped it turban-style around her hair.

"But I have no makeup on, no—!" Harper shot again and again.

Then Harper called everyone back to gather around

the loveseat with their Manchester Linens products visible, and took another series of photos.

"How come Dillon doesn't have to do this?" Darrick wanted to know.

"Because you're all going home this afternoon, and I can shoot him anytime."

"Mmm," Darrick said. "Shoot him once for me. But no film. Use buckshot."

Dori whipped him with the towel she held.

Dillon had always known his family was special, but he felt a particular pang when the photo session finished, and they all dispersed in a hubbub of activity to pack the Lexus and the motor home and go off in their different directions again.

These times were precious, he knew. His parents had established a wonderful foundation for their children, and it was only now that he knew firsthand how difficult it could sometimes be to give and accept love that he realized they'd made the monumental task look easy.

Darrick caught him in the kitchen while everyone else was outside at the cars. "How's it going with Harper?" he asked. "Looks like the two of you resolved whatever it was."

"Well..." Dillon nodded. "Pretty much."

"You two have some big-time baggage, but love *can* win out."

Dillon wasn't anxious to share the details of his relationship, but he knew Darrick's questions were motivated by concern and not curiosity.

"We're trying hard." Dillon put an arm around his shoulders and walked him toward the front door. "Now, why don't you go home?" he teased. "And where's the dog? Don't forget the dog."

"He's already in the car. Dillon..."

"Darrick, don't preach to me, okay? It's going to be fine."

"Maybe," Darrick said gravely. "But it's not going to happen miraculously. You're going to have to make it be fine."

They proceeded down to the end of the walk, where David was being hugged by his grandparents.

"I thought I'd just leave it to Olivia," Dillon continued. "Harper's convinced Olivia sent the dress to make our relationship work out."

Darrick nodded. "You can blame Skye for that one. She's the one spreading the romantic-ghost virus. Just remember what I told you."

"Always carry protection?"

Darrick slapped the suitcase into his gut. "Call me if you need me," he corrected. "Hold this while I unlock the trunk."

"Are you coming back for the Fourth?" Dillon asked as his parents climbed into the motor home parked behind Darrick's Lexus. Harper and Dori had already said their goodbyes, each wearing a twin in a front pack, and Harper holding Darian by the hand. Dori helped, one-handed, as Skye and David redistributed David's gifts in the back seat of the car.

His mother nodded. "We're going to eastern Washington for the Motor Home Mavericks Roundup," she said, "and we'll head home just in time to hit you on Fourth of July weekend." She grinned. "It'd be nice if we came home to a wedding."

Wouldn't it?

"Hold the good thought," he said, standing on the running board and leaning in to kiss her goodbye. "We have to work out a few things first."

Charlie reached across his wife to shake Dillon's hand. "Understandable. Your mother's always excited about additions to the family. I think she's getting bonus points for them, or something. See you about the second or third."

"Right."

The motor home backed out of the driveway and was gone with a honk of the horn. Dillon picked up Darian and told him to wave.

There was another round of hugs with Darrick and Skye and David, and then they, too, were gone.

Harper shaded her eyes and watched until the Lexus disappeared. She sighed and slung an arm around Dori's shoulders. "I'm beginning to think you're right about buying up a block so we can all live near each other. Only not in Edenfield. Here in Dancer's Beach."

She smiled at Dillon. "This place is magic."

"Is it?" He and Darian got between Harper and Dori and led them toward the house. "Well, let's see if it'll make the breakfast dishes disappear."

"TAKE THE PAJAMA TOP OFF," Harper instructed, as Dillon prepared to join Darian and the babies on the bed made with Manchester Linens sheets. She stood behind her camera set on a tripod and gave directions like some tiny blond Spielberg.

Dillon complained quietly because the babies had fallen asleep after a long, fussy period, and Darian was looking drowsy. "Look. I don't even wear pajamas, but I put on these yuppy gray silk things you bought to make you happy, and now you want me to take them off?"

"Just the top," she said. Then she waggled her eyebrows. "At least until later. And that's only *if* you do a good job."

He pretended indignation. "To think my life has come to this—invitations to the casting room couch."

Harper leaned a hand on the camera and rolled her eyes. "Save the dramatics for when you're in front of the lens—and take the damn top off."

Forced to cooperate because he sensed the if-you-do-a-good-job offer might be genuine, he tossed the pajama top aside, lay on the bed and followed her instructions.

She posed him with the twins lying on one side of him, and Darian on the other; then with them in his arms, lying on his chest, across his stomach, all in the crook of one arm...

"Oh, that's a winner," she said softly from behind the camera, and took four shots.

The twins slept on contentedly, worn out from the busy holiday and their fussy afternoon. Dillon put them in their portable crib, while Harper took a sleepy Darian and rocked him until he drifted off. Then she put him in his crib and put away her camera equipment.

Finished, she presented herself at the side of the bed, where Dillon sat propped against the pillows.

"Okay," she said, holding up the pajama top. "Do you want to put this back on, or take off the—"

He pulled her down on top of him before she could finish the question.

LIFE WAS IDYLLIC for ten long days.

The babies were now learning to turn over, to swipe at nearby objects and to vocalize. Had Harper not known better, she'd have sworn they were related to her singing aunts. Darian loved being Dillon's shadow, and was visibly happier than the already cheerful child he'd always been.

Dillon and Harper put down new floor covering in the kitchen, painted Dori's bathroom and raced to Used But Enthused when the owner called to tell them he'd just gotten in a natural rattan set for the sunroom that included a sofa, a loveseat, two chairs and a coffee table.

They sat on the loveseat, the babies in their arms, and Darian trying out a matching chair, as they admired their find.

"I can't believe it's in such great condition!" Harper said.

"It's like it was meant for this porch." Dillon made faces at Michelle, who lay in his lap, her legs and feet propped up against his chest, her head in his hands. Gabrielle lay in the crook of Harper's arm, fast asleep. "This would be a great place to laze away a summer afternoon. Next summer'll be great here."

"You don't think this month's been great?" Harper asked.

"Sure it has," he replied, "but you have to admit we haven't had much time to laze. And Duncan's missed all the labor. He missed the painting and the furnishing, and will arrive with nothing left to do but garden."

"Gardening's hard work."

"Not for Duncan. He loves it."

"Have you heard from him?"

"No. He'll just come breezing in one day with a leggy blonde on his arm and stories about the nightlife in Budapest or the wildlife in the Outback."

"Do I detect a little jealousy?"

He grinned, stroking Michelle's downy head with

the tips of his fingers. "Damn right. He was the oldest, the one who could talk himself out of anything, and now he has the world's most glamorous women beating a path to his door in the world's most beautiful locations."

"But he has to play the villain. You get to be the good guy. The world probably appreciates you more."

Dillon gave her a disbelieving look. "The world appreciates his beautiful, evil face, and so do the high-living ladies who like to court danger."

"Dillon," Harper scolded, turning toward him. "You're the father of three children. You're not supposed to be thinking about high-living ladies who like to court danger."

"Why not?" he challenged. "You like to think about Barton and that he adventured off to the Klondike to find Olivia."

"That's different."

"How?"

"Olivia was good for him. High-living ladies are bad news."

He laughed. "How would you know?"

She patted her hair and heaved a bored sigh. "I used to be one, you know."

"Really? When?"

"When I worked on the twenty-seventh floor of the Frobisher Building in Los Angeles."

He groaned. "That's high-working, not high-living."

There was a moment of silence, then Harper asked interestedly, "Is Allison a high-living lady?"

"Not at all. Fast-living, maybe. And not in the sense of self-destructive habits, but of craving action and excitement. And danger."

"Danger," Harper repeated, then taunted drily. "So how come she didn't have babies with Duncan instead of you? If you're the good guy, what was it she found appealing about you?"

Dillon looked into her eyes, his own dark and direct and reading the mild annoyance in her. "I don't know. What is it you find appealing?"

"The twins," she teased. "But you didn't have them when you met Allison."

"I didn't have them when you first found me appealing, either. It has to be something else."

"Okay. Your looks and your money."

He laughed. "Well, that's only fair. All I wanted was your body."

"Is it safe to come in here?" Dori asked from the doorway, apparently having overheard their exchange. "I mean, you're not going to do anything disgusting in front of the babies, are you?"

"Why not?" Dillon asked. "Gabrielle's asleep, and Michelle and Darian don't want to miss anything."

"Well, relax Romeo," she said, coming to take Michelle from him. "Chuck Bartomeo's on the phone."

Harper tensed as Dillon got up to take the call. Chuck Bartomeo was the Northwest Medical Team's contact person.

Dillon exchanged a look with her before he left the room. She forced a smile for him, feeling their idyllic month together slip away from her like the shells on the sand at high tide.

Dori took Dillon's place, bouncing Michelle as she fussed at the disturbance.

"It's probably that hurricane in Mexico," Dori said, studying Harper in concern. "I just saw on the news that a hospital collapsed and lots of the staff were injured.''

All the old grievances rose to haunt Harper. She guessed that it was his eagerness to go that always annoyed her the most.

''He's the absolute best there is,'' Dori said, as though guessing what she was thinking and trying to placate her.

''I know that,'' Harper said. ''He's a great doctor. But now he has three little babies.''

''We can take care of them until he comes back.''

Dillon was back in a surprisingly short time.

''When do you leave?'' Dori asked him.

He took Michelle back from her, and carried the infant to the window that surrounded the porch. ''I'm not going,'' he said.

Harper couldn't quite believe her ears.

Dori frowned, as though she also doubted what she'd heard. ''Why not?''

''I called Jerry Winter. He's going.''

Jerry Winter was one of his partners in the clinic.

Harper's initial reaction to that was delight, delirium. He'd actually made the decision that someone besides him was competent to respond to a crisis. He had chosen to stay home with his babies—and with her.

Her next reaction was guilt. He'd made the decision to send someone in his place because she'd condemned him over and over for running to the rescue in every health crisis across the globe.

''You're sure that's what you want to do?'' Harper crossed the room toward him.

''I'm sure.''

''And the group had no problem with that?''

''None at all. Jerry's excellent.''

The discussion continued on and off through dinner and while they were getting ready for bed. Dori was asleep in her attic aerie, Darian in his crib across the hall. The babies had just nodded off.

Dillon came out of the bathroom in the cotton T-shirt and the boxers he always wore to bed.

Harper, in a short, thin nightie, sat propped up against her pillows, watching him look into the crib at the babies, adjust their blanket, then stroke each little head.

He'd been amiable all evening, betraying no evidence of disappointment or regret over his decision to stay home.

Guilt consumed her.

"Dillon," she said softly, as he turned off the bedside lamp, "about Mexico."

"It's settled, Harper." She felt the mattress shift as it took his weight. His arm brushed against her, then the cotton of his shirt, his foot.

"You want to go."

"I'll always want to go. That's not the point."

"What is the point?"

"I have three children. I should be home with them."

"I'll feel awful if you ignore people in pain and in need because I have this…security thing."

"Put your mind at rest," he said, settling down into the darkness beside her. "I'm staying because of the babies, not because of you."

"You're lying."

"Did I ever stay home for you before?"

"No."

"All right, then." He pulled her close and kissed her temple. "Go to sleep."

She did, and her last thought as sleep claimed her was that this *was* a magical place. She'd never have believed this day would come.

Chapter Twelve

The call that changed everything came at breakfast. Harper answered it, carrying Michelle in the front pack. It was Jerry Winter over a very poor connection.

Harper handed the phone to Dillon, who carried the other twin. Darian sat on his knees on a chair eating Cheerios one by one.

Harper guessed what the call meant even before Dillon glanced at her with a grave expression.

"Well, why are there so many?" he asked. Then he answered feelingly, "Jesus!" He listened a while longer, then said abruptly, "Hold on." He handed Dori the baby, then scribbled on the yellow pad on which she'd been at work over breakfast. Then, with an eagerness in his voice that Harper always recognized before a trip, he said, "Right. I'll be there as soon as I can. Yeah. I'll let you know."

"What happened?" Dori asked.

Dillon broke the connection, then tucked the pad under his arm and stabbed out a number. "Lots of casualties under twelve. The pediatrics wing of the hospital that collapsed sustained the most damage. Sick children with broken bones are enough to destroy any doctor's faith in himself. Jerry wants help. Hi, Janie?

Dillon. Yeah, I know they did. I'm on my way to join them. Can you get me a reservation as soon as possible? And can you get Air-Docs to pick me up here and take me to Portland Airport? Thanks. Of course. Double your salary and add a bonus. A yacht? I don't know, that's a little optimistic. Settle for a canoe and you've got it. Okay. Thanks, Janie.''

Dillon cradled the wall phone and turned back to the table.

Dori and Gabrielle sat alone.

''Harper went to pack you a bag,'' Dori replied to his unspoken question.

Dillon took Gabrielle with him upstairs, where Harper had the battered garment bag that had been with him all over the globe. Darian was removing things from it almost as quickly as Harper put them in. She reclaimed and replaced each item.

''The team will have your scrubs and instruments?'' Harper asked without slowing her pace from closet to bed. She worked like an automaton, her movements hurried but efficient, her face expressionless.

''Right,'' he replied. She'd placed Michelle in the crib, so he put Gabrielle down beside her.

He caught Harper on her way back to the closet and pulled her to a stop, drawing her to him, looping his arms around her. She didn't resist, but she was far from pliable.

''I'm sorry,'' he said. ''But this is a unique situation.''

She nodded. ''I know. I understand completely.''

Dillon looked into her eyes and saw that she did. But there was something turbulent in them beneath the understanding.

He felt both sympathy for her and frustration for

himself. Even after all they'd learned about each other over the last few weeks, this part hadn't changed. When he had to leave her to join the medical team, the same tension crackled between them that had split them up two years ago. He felt defeated and angry—not a good frame of mind for setting little bones and mending little bodies.

Darian, seeming to sense the tension and perhaps the imminent departure, wrapped himself around Dillon's leg. "Da-da!" he said in a demanding tone.

Dillon picked him up.

"I understand," Harper said as she went to the closet and pulled out his boots. "But he doesn't. And I don't know how to explain it to him." She put one boot in one side pocket, and one in the other.

Dillon's annoyance with her wavered as he realized that she hadn't forgotten the packing drill.

"Maybe he'll understand when I come back—" Dillon followed her as far as the bathroom door when she marched into the little room "—that even though I have to be gone, my return means my commitment is total."

She pulled his shaving kit out of a drawer and dropped in toothpaste and deodorant. Then she marched past him back to the case.

"He is a little genius," she conceded, putting the kit in the pocket where Dillon always placed it. "But I think it's just going to feel to him as though his wonderful new daddy is gone."

That felt as though she'd gut-punched him. "Thanks," he said. "That's a great way to send me off."

She stopped her frantic but efficient movements to stand toe to toe with him. "Deal with it, Dillon," she said mercilessly. "You go off on your heroic jaunts, and I'm supposed to put my life on hold while you're gone. Maybe you can ask that of me, but you can't expect Darian not to feel the loss."

He wanted to bellow at her, but Darian—unused to this discord—was already starting to cry.

"There are scores of little children—" he began, desperate to make her understand, and to absolve himself of guilt.

"I know that." She nodded wearily. "This is a unique situation. I'm just reminding you that for all the times it isn't, for all the times someone else could handle it for you—" she indicated the baby now crying in his arms and clinging to his neck "—this is how he's going to feel. And the girls, too, when they're old enough."

He rocked Darian from side to side, surprised by the child's death-grip on him. It was a life-grip, really. He felt it in the twins all the time. Babies knew what they needed, and held on to it.

He said the only thing he could think of that would make her as responsible for this horrible moment as he was.

"I'm not his *new* daddy," he snapped at her. "I'm his *old* daddy. Thanks to you, he doesn't know that. He thinks I just arrived!"

She yanked his bag off the bed and dragged it to the door, ignoring his last remark. Then she reached her hands out for the now-screaming baby, wincing against the sound.

"I'll take him. You'll have to carry the bag."

He didn't answer, but started out the door with the bag in one hand and Darian in the other arm.

"Dill?" Dori appeared beside him.

"What?" he snarled at her.

"Sorry. I know it's not the right moment, but Air-Docs called and said to tell you they'll pick you up at Foxglove Field in fifteen minutes. Janie got you a flight that leaves PDX at 11:00 a.m."

He nodded apologetically. "Thanks, Dori."

"Sure. I'll drive you."

"Great."

He followed Dori down the stairs, telling Darian all the while that he was going to be gone but that he was coming back.

Harper had to peel Darian from him at the truck.

The baby reached out for him and Dillon was stunned by how much that hurt. He kissed Darian and told him again that he'd be back. But he knew, of course, that the boy didn't understand.

Dillon looked into Harper's eyes and saw her pain, and the pain she felt for her son. "We'll talk when I get back," he said.

She nodded, trying to control the baby pushing against her, trying to get to his father. "Okay," she said, but he heard the futility in her voice. They'd talked and talked, and nothing had ever changed.

As Dori drove off, Dillon looked in the side mirror and saw Harper's cheek pressed against his screaming son's. He knew then that this time something *had* to change.

HARPER AND DORI MADE A PACT. Harper tended Darian and the twins all morning, while Dori worked on her thesis. She was close to having the rough draft finished and her eyes were bright with excitement at the prospect.

Then Dori watched the babies all afternoon, while

Harper attached the silk skirt she'd made to the bodice of Olivia's dress. She'd made peace with her feelings of uneasiness in the attic. If Dori could be there alone and not be nervous, then so could she.

Harper half expected mist to swirl or stars to fall when she pierced the bodice with her needle to baste the skirt onto it—but nothing happened. Sun streamed through the attic window and dust swirled in the shaft of light. But nothing moved.

The big stitches in place, Harper fluffed out the skirt and stepped back to study it. It looked just as it might have a century ago, had Olivia been able to finish it.

"All right," Harper said, perching on the foot of Dori's bed. "So, Skye was wrong. The dress wasn't intended to help me. But maybe it'll do something for Dori." She tried to imagine Dori with her degree in hand and some brilliant Regency period novel underway, walking up the aisle in the dress toward a handsome young man waiting at the front of the church. Her mind placed Salvatore Dominguez there. She smiled to herself.

She stood again, bracing herself for the next step in completing the dress. It had to come off the dress form so that she could take it to her room and actually hand-stitch the skirt to the bodice.

She stood behind the bodice and put her fingers to the long row of tiny pearl buttons attached by a long row of little loops. The first loop was a tight fit and resisted her efforts, but finally slipped off its pearl button.

Again, nothing magical happened.

Harper was almost disappointed. Then she fixed the picture of Dori in her mind, walking up the aisle to some handsome young man, and decided that love—

when it worked—was indeed magical. And maybe Dori would find it.

She worked all the loops carefully. Then, all the buttons undone, she placed her hands under the skirt and pushed gently upward from inside the bodice. Suddenly the dress was up and off the form. Harper draped it carefully over her arm, then took it to the bed where she'd opened out a clean sheet. She wrapped the dress in the sheet, then carried it down the ladder to Duncan's room.

She tried unsuccessfully not to think about Dillon. She and Dori distracted Darian with games and new toys—but she couldn't distract herself. She missed him terribly, and loneliness made all that stood between them monumental.

This trip had become such an issue because of Darian's reaction that the matter of the twins' mother had been pushed into the background. But what if Allison Cartier *did* want Dillon back when he finally reached her?

Allison might seem like a relief to him after the frustration Harper had caused him.

"HARPER!"

Harper lay the dress in the middle of Duncan's bed and turned at the anxious sound of Dori's voice.

"What?" she asked in the same tone, her first thought going to the babies. "What's wrong?"

"Ah...nothing," Dori said, pointing toward the stairs.

"Are the kids all right?"

"They're fine. But you should come down. There are five women with suitcases in the middle of the living room singing 'Scarlet Ribbons.'"

"What?" Harper started for the stairs.

Strains of the beautiful old song greeted her at the top of the stairs, the harmony full and round and perfect.

Her aunts! A cheering excitement filled her and she ran down the steps to find the five women standing in the middle of the room. Aunt Phyl was on crutches, Aggie and Cleo held the babies. Edith and Grace, who still sang together professionally, were arm in arm, eyes closed, lost in the music. Darian stood on the sofa, Grace's arm around him.

As the last note faded away, Harper screamed and leapt into the circle of songsters.

Confusion reigned for a full five minutes. Harper hugged and embraced each one, while they all tried to tell her at once what they'd been up to and why they were here.

They constituted a bevy of attractive and energetic women of late middle age. Aggie, the eldest, was fifty-nine, small, and wore her graying blond hair in a very short cut. She was a performing artist's representative.

Aunt Phyl had done voice-overs for television, but now contented herself with Edenfield's community theater. She was fifty-six and still looking for Mr. Right.

"We're all headed for New York in a week or so," Cleo said, after telling Harper about her visit with her publisher. "Edith and Grace auditioned for the parts of a pair of maiden aunts in *Portraits in a Penthouse* on Broadway—and got the parts!"

"You're kidding!" Harper hugged Edith and then Grace. "But I thought clubs were your thing!"

Edith, the most beautiful of all the aunts, still had the elegant bone structure and coltish build of her girlhood. "It was Aggie's suggestion. She heard about the audition and suggested we try. We figured, why not? You're never too old to try something new.''

Grace was the sweet one, and the youngest. She was a little plump, very pretty, and was said to have had her heart broken by a trumpet player when she was twenty.

"So now we're having our Broadway debuts—'' she squeezed Darian between herself and Edith ''—at fifty-three and fifty-five.''

Harper put a hand to her heart. "My aunts on Broadway. I can't believe it!''

"We were hoping you could come with us,'' Cleo said. "We're just going to drop them off and do some sightseeing and shopping.''

Then Cleo noticed Dori lingering on the fringe of their boisterous group and caught her arm, pulling her inside. "Who are you, dear? Dillon's sister?''

"Yes, I'm Dori,'' she said, smiling a little nervously around the group. "I'm a sort of nanny around here.''

"Yes.'' Phyl, leaning on her crutches, winked at Harper. "I remember you saying something about twins when we spoke on the phone. These beautiful babies are Dillon's?''

"Well, we think so,'' Harper said.

Five pairs of eyes turned to her in confusion.

Harper shooed them all toward chairs. "I'll tell you what. You sit, and Dori and I'll get some coffee and goodies underway. Then I'll explain everything—or, at least what I know.'' She turned to Dori. "Is there any problem with putting them up for a few days?''

Dori frowned at her. "Of course not. And for even asking that, you can fix the coffee and goodies while I get them settled. Aunt Phyl can stay down here in

Mom and Dad's room, then she won't have to negotiate the stairs with her crutches.''

The aunts holding the babies didn't want to part with them and brought them along as they followed Dori.

Harper found herself standing alone in the kitchen with Darian, who started to help by pulling all of the plastics out of the bottom cupboard.

Harper brewed coffee, poured it into a warming carafe, then brewed another pot. She set the dining room table with a single bedsheet, and blessed Bertie, who was keeping them supplied with cookies; she put the sweets on a plate in the middle of the table. Then she went to check on Phyl's progress.

She found her aunt lying on her back on the bed. Darian had joined her with a bowl and a spoon.

''I'm fine,'' she assured Harper, who sat beside her in concern. ''It's just that with all my sisters trying to take care of me and see that I'm not bored, I've done more traveling since I've had knee replacement surgery than I did before it!'' She laughed at the absurdity. Then she frowned suddenly. ''I suppose Dillon's off to Mexico. I heard on the news that the Northwest Medical Team had been called up.''

Harper nodded and explained about the pediatrics wing of the hospital that had collapsed.

Phyl groaned empathetically. ''How awful.'' Then she patted her leg. ''I tell you, for those of us who need them, it's one of God's miracles that there are doctors who can make us whole again. I felt so helpless when I had to hobble around and lean on other people.'' She laughed again and rolled her eyes. ''Of course, I still do that and will until I'm completely healed. But once I am, I'll be independent again. Imagine what that's like for little children who should be able to run and jump and play.'' She cupped Darian's cheek with a slender hand. ''Doctors like Dillon are a blessing.''

Harper nodded and forced a smile, then helped Phyl to her feet. ''Yes, they are.'' She handed her a crutch. ''Come on. You can have first pick of the cookies. Come on, Dare-devil.''

Phyl pulled against her as she started to lead her from the room. Harper turned back to see her aunt watching her speculatively. ''Have you two made up?''

Harper didn't want to spoil this cheerful reunion. ''Oh, you know us,'' she said lightly, tugging on Phyl. ''On again, off again. The usual.''

''So are you on or off right now? You look a little fishy.''

''Fishy?''

''Tricky. This conversation is like you're darting in and out of rocks, but I can see you through the clear water.''

''Goodness, what a metaphor.''

''Don't try to distract me. On or off?''

''Sort of in between,'' she said brightly. Then, when Phyl didn't seem convinced, she added, ''Okay, off mostly.''

''Because he went with the team?''

Phyl had always been on Dillon's side in the past. ''Because I think he's more comfortable, even happier, with the team than he is with me.''

Phyl shook her head. ''Darling, it isn't that he's happier with them. It's that he has to use his gift. Just as you have to use yours. Certainly you know that.''

Harper sighed and patted Phyl's hand, trying desperately not to lose the glimpse of cheer her aunts' arrival had brought her. ''I do. It's just that I don't think I can live with it, Aunt Phyl. I like my little cocoon of comfort and safety. And Darian got so close to Dillon, and then had a fit when he left.''

''Oh, babies can have a fit when a parent goes to the store.'' Phyl allowed herself to be led out into the kitchen. ''But,'' she added, ''I know how you are. I also know that, however innocently, we did that to you—your other aunts and I.''

Harper would have died rather than hurt any of them. ''Of course you didn't,'' she said firmly, leading Phyl to the dining room. ''Mom and Dad and I were such a tight little unit that losing them at that age made me feel as though all my protections had been neutralized. I was very frightened. But you and your sisters welcomed me with open arms. That was wonderful.''

Phyl sat in the chair Harper pulled out for her. ''But then with our busy lives we moved you from one pair of open arms to the other, and for a girl trying to grow roots again, that wasn't a good thing.''

''Nonsense.''

''No, it's true.'' Phyl sighed and stared thoughtfully, eyes unfocused. ''You came into our childless lives, and we were all so excited to be able to share you. It didn't occur to us then that moving about was probably all very unsettling for you.''

Harper began to deny again that they'd done anything harmful while they'd cared for her, but the other aunts and Dori returned with Michelle and Gabrielle and the very numbers prevented Harper and Phyl from continuing their conversation.

But Harper thought about it all evening while they ate Chinese take-out; exchanged favorite stories from their long careers in the music business; pumped Dori for details about her studies and what she hoped to do with them; and asked about the absent McKeons. Each baby sat in a welcoming lap.

"I wish Duncan would make a musical," Grace said with a dreamy flick of her eyelashes. "I'd convince him how great life could be with an older woman." Then she giggled.

Her sisters alternately laughed and gasped.

"You were always the most spoiled!" Cleo accused good-naturedly. "That's why you're such a risk-taker today."

"It's the youngest-child thing," said Phyl, always the philosopher. "Like Dillon McKeon, going to the wilds of the world and putting himself in the path of unknown and unchecked danger. Probably trying to prove himself as good as his older siblings."

Aggie made a scornful sound. "That's not true in Gracie's case. She's just a brat. And what have we accomplished that she hasn't? She's going to be on Broadway!"

"Well, that's now," Phyl explained patiently. "The reckless thing began when we were children and she started a pattern of behavior she just can't stop." She grinned at Gracie. "Next thing you know, she'll be getting a tattoo and piercing her navel."

Gracie stood and lifted her skirt. "I already have a tattoo. See?"

Visible through her sheer panty hose was a small butterfly on a dimpled thigh. She tightened her muscle, then relaxed it; it looked as though the butterfly flapped its wings.

There was much laughter, and Harper felt as though at least one layer of the pall over her life had been lifted.

Michelle and Gabrielle, she thought an hour later,

were probably the only babies in the world to be serenaded to sleep by the magical harmony of an aging but still elegant quintet. Edith and Grace held the babies in the middle of the sofa, and their sisters all gathered around, singing about sandmen and dreamlands and cradles in treetops.

"I'm chucking my studies," Dori leaned over to Harper to whisper, "and I'm going on the road with them. Have you ever in your life seen five more fun ladies?"

Harper shook her head. "Never."

Dori sighed. "Losing your parents must have been awful, but what a wonderful net you fell into."

"Yes." *You came into our childless lives, and we were all so excited to be able to share you.* Phyl's words played over in Harper's mind. And as Dori focused on the aunts and they sang on, Harper thought back on that period of her life.

As a young teen, she'd been shocked and hurt by her parents' death, and she'd been understandably self-involved, like most girls that age.

But she was now old enough to appreciate that five women with busy careers had made room in their lives for their sister's child when it would have been so much easier for them to have disregarded their responsibilities—or to have left them to one or the other of the sisters exclusively.

But each had pitched in to do her part—they'd all done their best to try to help ground her again.

For the first time, she clearly saw a parallel between herself and the twins. Her parentage wasn't a mystery, but she'd moved from one pair of loving hands to another while her life was sorted out.

How fortunate they all were to have such a store-house of love to support them.

Edith and Gracie put the babies to bed in the cribs Harper had moved to Duncan's room. Then Dori, who was now in thick with the aunts, told them about the things Olivia had ''left'' in the attic.

Harper brought the dress down to show them, and told them the story of the Buckley brothers and the dancers who'd been shipwrecked off the shore. She told them about Bertie giving her the fabric, and about Fran and the things she'd found in the basement of the hotel.

''Well, let's see that stuff,'' Aggie ordered, shooing Harper toward the stairs. ''Maybe there's a clue.''

''She's been over it and over it...'' Dori began.

But the aunts were adamant. Harper brought it all down and the aunts pored over the things spread out on the coffee table. Dori and Harper knelt on the floor.

The photos, the invoice, the hairpin and ribbon, the recipe—all were passed from hand to hand, then came back to Aggie, who looked at one of the photos more closely.

Cleo leaned closer to her. ''What do you see, Aggie?''

''Well. I'm not sure.'' She slipped her glasses up onto her head and squinted at the photograph. ''But...look at this christening dress.''

She held the photo down so that everyone could look at it. Harper and Dori had to crane their necks. Then Aggie had to slip her glasses down again. ''Look at the beading on the baby's dress.''

Seven heads closed to bumping distance.

''I don't even see beading,'' Cleo complained.

"Cleo, you're blind as a bat. Where are your reading glasses? Stop being prideful and put them on."

The photo was passed on down the sofa while Cleo took the criticism gracefully and dug into her purse.

Harper ignored the commotion as the photo came around to her and Dori. She held it up as Dori leaned in.

And then she saw it. A faint V-pattern line on the long skirt of the baby's gown. It was barely discernible in the photo, but it was exactly the same pattern of beading as on the bodice.

Harper and Dori looked at each other. "Coincidence?" Dori whispered.

Harper studied it again, her heartbeat accelerating. "I don't know."

"It was common then," Aggie said, "to make the baby's christening gown out of the mother's wedding dress."

"But..." Dori sat back on her heels. "It clearly wasn't made out of the bodice, and it *had* no skirt..."

"Because it was made into a christening dress," Harper breathed.

Aggie examined the dress they'd rewrapped and placed on the loveseat. Everyone got up to crowd around her—Phyl with her crutches, and Cleo with her reading glasses.

"It's more difficult to tell with hand-stitching," Aggie said. "It doesn't leave the nice tidy trail of little holes that machine-stitching does. And good seamstresses were artists with a needle. They replaced sleeves and hems and panels so that you'd never know they weren't original. But, *there*..." She had turned the bodice inside out so that they could study the bottom, and the very small, almost invisible holes in the fabric that indicated a skirt had long ago been attached to it.

"She *did* get married!" Harper whispered to Dori.

Dori pointed to the photo on the coffee table. "And she had her *baby!* Wait till we tell Skye!"

Dori snatched up the photo and brought it into their circle. "But, let's not get too excited here. We still have some unanswered questions." She pointed to the wedding photo. "Is this Olivia with Barton? And if this is their baby, where are they? Who are these two people? I don't recognize either of them from the Buckley family history."

"Well, it's probably godparents," Edith said.

Everyone turned to her in pleased surprise. "That's it! Godparents!" The cry was unanimous.

"But we don't know that for sure. We still have to identify these people." Harper frowned at the photo, feeling her enthusiasm slip. Then she remembered her new perspective. There was no definite proof that Olivia had married Barton and had had a baby, but someone *had* made a christening dress out of Olivia's wedding skirt.

They were a step closer to solving the mystery.

Gracie took the photos. "Edie and I played Anchorage in our younger days," she said with a grin. "And we have friends there. I'll call and see if they can check state and historical records for a Barton Buckley or Olivia Marbury. It's a chance in a million, but that's what I'll do."

Harper hugged her fiercely.

When everyone had gone to bed, Harper lay among her pillows and wondered how Dillon was. She imagined him in some poorly equipped hospital, putting a child's leg back together. She wondered selfishly if he'd even given her a passing thought.

Then she chided herself. His *every* thought should be on the injured children.

THE AUNTS HAD BEEN at Dancer's Beach for four days when Harper realized she'd never had so much free time. One or the other of the aunts was always cleaning, clearing away, feeding or bathing the babies, running for groceries, doing laundry.

They walked on the beach, went to town shopping, ate in the backyard, watched old movies, and generally enjoyed lazy summer days.

The twins were growing plump and spoiled by all the attention, and Darian had them all in the palm of his hand.

Harper felt herself relaxing, wallowing in her aunts' love. And she reflected on how different these few days had been from the way she'd expected to spend them when she and Dillon had parted so unhappily.

The aunts now talked about Olivia the same way she and Dori and Skye did, and that made her "ghost" seem even more real to Harper than ever.

While she'd been out with the aunts that morning, Dillon had called and told Dori, who'd stayed home to work, that he'd be home July second. The day after tomorrow.

"What kind of shells do you want for this project?" Aggie asked.

Harper had hung fabric ribbon from the curtain rod in the kitchen window with the fanciful idea of attaching shells to the ribbon as a way to bring the beach indoors on gloomy winter days.

"Whatever you can find," Harper replied. The aunts

were all dressed in jeans and sweats for their shell-gathering expedition—except Phyl, who was staying home and napping to rest her knee.

"Why don't *you* go with them?" Dori suggested to Harper.

"No." Harper turned Dori around and pushed her to follow the group. "You've been studying all day. You need fresh air. Sand dollars, scallop shells, clam shells, anything. Just bring back lots in case I screw up."

Harper closed the door behind the expedition. Then she went to ask Phyl to join her in a cup of tea, but her aunt was already asleep. Harper closed her door and decided the make a pot for herself.

She filled the kettle and turned it on, while the twins snoozed contentedly in the portable crib on the sun-porch, and Darian dozed on the sofa.

The doorbell distracted Harper from a search for cookies. The aunts' sweet tooth had done a number on the treat supply.

Wondering if one of her aunts had come back for a jacket, Harper pulled open the door—and felt her heart leap into her throat. She found herself face to face with a gorgeous redhead.

Allison Cartier.

Chapter Thirteen

"I'm looking for Dillon McKeon."

Even if Harper hadn't recognized Allison's face, she'd have recognized the beautifully formed tones, the perfect diction, and the look that was direct and confident and somehow intimate, as though of the many millions of viewers watching her on television, you alone had her attention.

Her heart thumping with several strong and complex emotions, Harper opened the door wider and invited her inside.

"This is his home," Harper said, "but I'm afraid he's away at the moment."

Allison nodded. "The hurricane in Mexico? I thought so."

The two stood just inside the door studying each other. Allison extended her hand. "Allison Cartier. I'm a friend of Dillon's."

Harper shook her hand. "Harper Harriman. Also a friend. Have you just returned from Palestine?"

Allison raised a surprised eyebrow that was the same rich ginger color as her loose, shoulder-length hair. Masses of ringlets, which were probably natural rather than permed, framed a milky white complexion completely free of freckles.

She wore a blue chambray shirt and jeans that showed off her slender, leggy body to perfection. Over her shoulder was a huge, shapeless leather bag.

"Two days ago," Allison replied, slipping the bag off her shoulder. "I got stuck in the office before I even had a chance to check my messages." Her expression became concerned. "Is Dillon all right? The message to call him was almost a month old."

"He's fine," Harper reassured her, drawing her toward the kitchen. "Here, set your bag down and I'll make you a cup of coffee? Tea?"

"Tea would be wonderful." Allison followed her, then stopped, noticing Darian napping on the sofa under a paisley shawl. "Yours?" she asked.

"Yes," Harper replied, keeping to herself that he was also Dillon's.

Allison sighed wistfully, and Harper felt her heart give a jolt of alarm. "Aren't babies something?" Then she straightened again and looked around her as she trailed Harper into the kitchen. "What a wonderful old place."

Harper pointed her to a chair and Allison sat, angling one jeans-clad leg over the other as she looked around. "I always swear to myself I'm going to invest in a house rather than a condo, but I'm never there. Why are there ribbons on the curtain rod?"

Harper had filled the kettle and carried it to the stove. She smiled at Allison over her shoulder. "I saw it in a magazine. You drill holes in seashells with a jeweler's drill and hang them on the ribbon. My aunts and Dillon's sister are out collecting them right now."

"Ah. You all live here?"

"No. I'm—I've been vacationing for a few weeks, and my aunts just stopped in to see me on their way to New York. Dori lives here, though. That's Dillon's sister."

Allison nodded, turning her attention from the kitchen to Harper, who was staring woefully into an empty cookie tin.

"Nothing to go with the tea, I'm afraid." Harper showed Allison the bottom of the tin. "My aunts are like locusts where sweets are concerned."

Allison shook her head. "I ate at the airport. I suppose I should have called first, but I thought it would be fun to surprise Dillon." She grinned ruefully. "But he always turns the tables."

"He called this morning." Harper brought napkins and the sugar and creamer to the table. "He'll be in the day after tomorrow. I'm sure he'd love it if you stayed and waited for him. Then you can still surprise him."

Allison sighed. "Thank you, but I can't. I'm due in Dublin tomorrow."

Harper blinked. "How are you going to do that?"

Allison glanced at her watch. "I have a rented car, and I'm flying out of Portland Airport on the red-eye." She smiled again. "That's my life. From one airport to the other, and quick visits to friends in between who usually aren't there when I call."

"I'm sorry." Harper's sympathy was genuine. It sounded like an awful way to live, though Allison's appearance did nothing to substantiate that. She looked healthy and happy and quite wonderful.

Allison shrugged. "All part of the job. But I hate to have missed Dillon. You don't know what he wanted, do you?"

"Ah…" Harper felt her breath clog in her throat. This was something Dillon should handle personally— but he wasn't here, and Allison would be leaving shortly. "Actually…I do."

Allison waited expectantly.

Harper shifted nervously in her chair, then bounced up when the kettle whistled, grateful for the distraction. She put two tea bags in a fat brown pot and carried it and two mugs to the table.

Harper sat down again and the two looked at each other across the table. While Harper tried to form the question several times, Allison's gaze narrowed slightly and she finally folded her arms on the table and leaned toward Harper. "I'll bet you're the one," she said.

Sidetracked from her dilemma, Harper asked curiously, "What one?"

Allison's smile was gentle. "The last time I saw Dillon, he told me he was in love with a woman who didn't love him. I couldn't imagine anyone not loving him, so I guessed he was simply involved in a relationship he didn't understand. You're the other half of it, aren't you?"

Now Harper was startled as well as unable to ask the all-important question.

"I'm an investigative reporter," Allison said. "I'm suppose to see what people are trying to hide from me. Is it the absences you resent?"

It seemed futile to deny it. "Not the absences as much as the fact that he doesn't mind being away. I know he's devoted to his work, and I don't begrudge the people who need him, I just wish he understood that I need him, too." Harper leaned back in her chair, despondency slipping back into her reality and blackening her mood. "But that's kind of a moot point. We fought just before he left, and...I'm not sure there's much hope."

Allison studied her with mossy-green eyes that did seem to see deep inside her. But her manner was sympathetic rather than judgmental. "You know, if you could see him at work out there just once—" she leaned toward her over the table "—you'd see why he can't stay home. His surgical skill is remarkable, but he manages to quiet children who won't stop crying for anybody else, he comforts women and old men, the sick, the dying. He stands up to the bullies and bureaucrats who have no respect for their own people, and he finds medical supplies and food when everyone swears there's none to be had. He *cares,* Harper. Do you know what a precious quality that is in this world?"

"I do," Harper said sincerely, "I just want to feel secure in the knowledge that he cares that much for me."

"I think he does." Allison leaned back in her chair and took a sip of her tea. "You'd broken up with him when he and I connected in Zaire." Her beautiful brow furrowed and she shook her head. "I can't tell you how ugly that was. The machete injuries were horrific, doctors and nurses wept, but Dillon kept working and I kept shooting pictures. And then this wounded woman put her baby in my arms and it just...died." She expelled a ragged breath. "Dillon tried to bring her back, but she was gone. We turned to each other I think just to try to remember that somewhere in the world people touched each other with kindness."

Allison looked up at Harper, horrible memories in her eyes. Harper realized for the first time the emotional hazard inherent in reporting truth to a comfortable and complacent world. Television sanitized it for dinnertime consumption, but the reporter saw every ugly detail of it and was probably haunted by it for a lifetime.

"He can love you, Harper," she said gently. "But he can't make you secure in it. If you're not secure within yourself, he can't give that to you."

As Harper absorbed the unpalatable truth of that bit of wisdom, a high-pitched, indignant cry came from the portable crib on the sunporch.

Allison smiled and followed as Harper went to retrieve Michelle. "Yours? Oh, my goodness. Twins!"

Harper handed Allison the squalling baby, then picked up Gabrielle, who'd been awakened by her sister and was now shrieking her displeasure, too.

Together they carried the babies back into the kitchen. Harper peered out into the living room and saw with relief that Darian continued to nap. She warmed bottles in the microwave and handed one to Allison. They sat at the table again, babies effectively silenced.

"They're not mine," Harper said, bracing herself to finally blurt out the question. "We were wondering if they were yours."

Allison's eyes came up from their perusal of the baby she held to stare at Harper in astonishment. "Mine? What do you mean?"

Harper told her the long involved story of the twins being abandoned at the hospital with only D. K. McKeon listed as the father and a false name for the mother on the birth certificate.

Allison shook her head in bewilderment. "I can't believe Dillon thought I would do such a thing."

Harper hunched a shoulder. "The timing was right. You were the logical answer."

"Some day, when my need to know is satisfied, I might consider motherhood." Allison stroked Michelle's fuzzy tufts of hair. "Although I can't imagine that happening, but if it does, maybe I'd like to find an understanding man and have a baby. But I assure you these beautiful little bundles are not mine."

Harper ignored the relief coursing through her, because it didn't matter. The twins weren't Dillon's after all, but then, neither was she. She knew it would hurt him to learn that, and that caused her pain, too.

Allison was leaving just as the aunts and Dori returned from their shell hunt. Harper made introductions and there was much laughter and excitement as Allison greeted them. Then Allison climbed into her rental car and backed out of the driveway. Everyone waved her off.

"She isn't the twins' mother," Harper whispered to Dori as they trailed the aunts into the house.

Dori nodded. "I know."

"Then…the babies have to be Duncan's."

Dori closed her eyes. "I hadn't thought of that." She looked heavenward in supplication. "God. Here we go again."

DILLON WALKED OUT of the Sangre de Cristo Hospital outside of Tampico, Mexico, with an entourage of doctors and nurses with whom he'd worked for the past eight days. Dr. Nikanor Sandoval, the chief of surgery with whom Dillon had worked closely, gave him an effusive hug. The man was a head shorter than he was and almost as wide, but he had the love and compassion of a kindred spirit.

"I cannot tell you what you have given us—" his eyes brimmed "—what you've given the children. I would not have thought a week ago that they would all walk again one day. But they will. Thank you."

Dillon shook his hand. "You're welcome, Nikanor. Come and see me when you visit your brother in the States."

"I will, I promise."

Another hug, a chorus of thanks and goodbyes from the rest of the group, and Dillon strode across the street to where Darrick and Skye waited with a rented Jeep. It was a ten-minute drive to the airport.

"It was very thoughtful and generous of you guys to freight supplies over yourselves, then to wait to bring me home." He slapped Darrick's shoulder from the back seat.

"Happy to." Darrick glanced at him in the mirror. "Mom and Dad were thrilled to watch David as long as we made sure you were back in time for the Fourth."

Dillon let a moment pass, then asked with practiced casualness, "Is Harper still there?"

Darrick now frowned into the mirror. "What do you mean?"

"You haven't been in touch with the beach house?"

"No." Darrick now glowered into the mirror. "What did you do?"

"Nothing," Dillon denied, irritated that Darrick would think to blame him without even knowing what had happened. "Why does it have to be my fault?"

"Because where Harper's concerned, it usually is. What happened?"

"We had a fight, that's all," Dillon said. "Nothing new with us. I got the call to come to Mexico, and you know how she is about that. Then Darian got really upset when I left and it all sort of…fell apart.''

"Yes," Skye said, glancing at him over her shoulder. "She doesn't resent your going as much as she resents your eagerness to get away."

Dillon huffed impatiently.

Darrick patted Skye's knee. "I'll handle it, Skye."

"Anyway, we yelled at each other and I just…wondered if she'd—I thought she might go." Dillon studied the passing scenery, all swamps and lagoons with the high-rises of Tampico in the distance. "Not that it's any of your business. I just wondered if she'd left."

"Would serve you right." Darrick turned into the small airport and drove the Jeep up to a little stucco building with a car rental sign.

Skye cast a disappointed look at Dillon, then turned to Darrick. "I'll just be a few minutes. I'll meet you guys in the plane."

Darrick carried Dillon's heavy bag in one hand and the small one he and Skye had brought in the other. When Dillon tried to take his bag, Darrick shook him off.

"Let me do you this favor," he said, walking toward an old Grumman with amphibious pontoons. "Because once I get our gear stowed, I'm going to tell you a few truths about yourself."

Dillon did an about-face and started to walk away.

Darrick dropped the heavy bag, caught his arm and pulled him back. "You're not going to escape this—so just relax."

"Who in the hell do you think—?" Dillon began, yanking out of his grip.

"Your loving brother," Darrick said drily, unlocking the baggage compartment door on the side of the plane. "And I didn't put up with you all those years so that you can wimp out on us now that you're finally getting to be interesting. Give me the bag."

Dillon slammed the heavy bag into him. Darrick held his stance and lifted it into the bay. Then he added his own small bag, closed the door and locked it.

Darrick turned to Dillon, hands on his hips.

Dillon squared off, two feet away, hands at his sides. "Harper is none of your business," he said in a low, threatening voice.

"Harper's a friend," Darrick returned quietly, "and you have to stop treating her as though you can pull her into your life, then push her out of it as it suits you. Or you're going to lose her. And I'd hate to see that happen to you."

"She left *me* two years ago."

"What choice did you give her?"

Dillon shifted his weight, resisting the urge to swing a fist at Darrick. He didn't want to have this conversation, but he also didn't want to spend Fourth of July weekend in Tampico.

"She kept my son a secret!" Dillon said angrily. "She hates my work!"

Darrick shook his head. "No, she doesn't. She hates that part of yourself you can't give her because it's still making reparations to Donovan."

Anger rose in Dillon like fire up a pine tree and he finally let his fist fly.

Darrick was ready for it, blocked the punch, caught his shirt collar and pushed him up against the plane.

"What are you doing?!" Skye shrieked, running toward them. She tried to push between them, pulling at Darrick's arms.

"Get in the plane," Darrick told her, tightening his hold on Dillon.

"Darrick!"

"Skye, get in the plane," Darrick ordered again, enunciating for emphasis. "This is between Dillon and me."

"Oh, like I'm not involved?" She folded her arms, her upper body still insinuated between the men.

"Skye, get in the plane," Dillon said reasonably.

She turned on him in hurt surprise. "I'm defending you!"

"I can defend myself. Get in the plane!"

"Well, maybe I will," she shouted into Darrick's face, then turned and shouted into Dillon's, "and maybe I'll just fly out of here and leave you both to find your own way home!"

She walked around the plane, and there was the sound of her door opening and the mild movement of the plane as she climbed in. The door slammed.

Darrick tightened his fist on the front of Dillon's shirt. "Are you listening to me?" he asked grimly.

Dillon told himself that he could have taken his brother. A few of the moves he'd learned over the years applied with care and determination and he could have his brother on the ground in a minute. They were evenly matched for height and weight, but he was almost three years younger.

But something prevented him from trying, and he wasn't sure what it was. He *was* sure that it wasn't a need to know what Darrick had to say.

"You've got your fist on my jugular," he replied, "and your ugly mug in my face. It's hard to do otherwise."

"Good. Then pay attention because I don't want to

dredge this up any more than you do. Only you're not pulling out of it on your own, so I'll yank you out." Darrick dropped his hand, folded his arms over his chest and leaned his weight on one hip.

"You're trying to save the world because there was nothing you could do to save Donovan. And you're always first on the spot of one disaster after another because you're trying to outrun the memory. Well, you can't. He was little and wonderful and he died. We were all powerless to do anything. You and Duncan and I were all too young to have to lose somebody like that, and it branded all of us in different ways. Little kids think they're responsible for everything, and there's something about holding the blame that helps you hold the person, but you have to let it go, Dill. I'm telling you to let it go."

Dillon was still flattened against the side of the plane. Darrick had freed him, but he was now pinned there by the partial truth of what his brother had said. Even Darrick didn't know all of it.

"Remember when he was bald?" Dillon asked, his throat constricting as he recalled the frail, skeletal figure his child-brother had become. "And too weak to get out of bed? And he'd want us to stay and play with him?"

He saw Darrick swallow. "I remember."

"Duncan read to him, you played games with him…" Dillon had to stop to draw a breath, to control his voice. "But I couldn't. It hurt too much to look at him. He wanted me to sit with him…and I couldn't."

"It was hard to look at him."

"I went to play in Jimmy Bristol's fort, instead. I felt like it protected me so I wouldn't get leukemia, too."

"You were just a little kid, Dillon."

"I know." Dillon's throat closed and tears brimmed in his eyes. "I know it's irrational, I just wish I could change it. He was…such a great kid."

A barbed sob caught in his throat.

To Dillon's horror, Darrick wrapped his arms around him. To his further horror, he found himself hanging on.

"Listen to me," Darrick said, his voice thick and shallow. "You did nothing wrong. You have nothing to make up for. I know your career is far more than reparation for Donovan, but I think you've made every extra moment a war between what you think you owe him, and the love you feel for Harper. She brightens your present and your future, and you're resisting that. Stop it. You can have it. You can be happy. Donovan died and it was awful—but we didn't."

Darrick tightened the hug, then let him go. He yanked open the copilot's door. "Now get in and lighten up or Skye's likely to dump us both somewhere where we'll never be found."

THERE WAS SOMETHING to be said for enlightenment. All the way home it warmed Dillon like sunlight on bare skin. But under the sudden freedom of it was the very real fear that it had come too late to save his future with Harper.

Skye and Darrick dropped him off at Foxglove Field.

"We're going to pick up Mom and Dad and David," Darrick said as he gestured to a cabbie, parked in front of the small terminal and eating a sandwich. "We'll be back in time for dinner so be sure to save some for us."

"All right." Dillon gave him a hug. "Thanks for

picking me up.'' He took a step toward the cab driving slowly in their direction, then looked Darrick in the eye. ''Both times,'' he added significantly.

Mercifully, Darrick didn't make a Kodak moment out of it. ''Sure. See you tonight.''

Dillon blew a kiss to Skye, who blew one back. He ran to the cab.

THERE WAS NO ONE HOME. *All right, don't panic,* Dillon told himself as he loped up the stairs. *It probably just means Harper and Dori have taken Darian and the twins for a walk on the beach or a trip to town. No cause for alarm.*

He reached the quiet hallway and walked down it with a sort of *Dead Man Walking* mindset. There *was* cause for alarm. When he'd left, all he'd promised had been a ''talk'' when he returned. And she'd been *there* before. She'd probably left just to save herself the aggravation of going through it all again.

She knew Skye and David would arrive tonight to help Dori with the twins. So she might have left with Darian rather than face dealing with another argument.

He wouldn't blame her.

He put his suitcase on the bed in his room, then walked reluctantly across the hallway to the room she'd used—Duncan's room—and scanned it for signs of occupancy: slippers, shoes she'd kicked off, an item of clothing on the bed.

There was nothing.

His hand feeling heavy, he pulled open her closet door. His heart slammed against his ribs when he saw the yawning emptiness. He put a hand to the molding on the door for support and told himself to breathe. But nothing seemed to be functioning. After that one punch inside him, his heart seemed to have stopped.

They were gone!

Hopelessness threatened to suck him down into sticky blackness, but he fought it, forcing himself to think. He knew where they'd gone. Seattle. He could go to Harper, explain what he'd learned about himself and them, and bring her and their son back. He closed his mind against the possibility that she no longer cared, that Darian had already forgotten.

He went into his room, snatched his cellular phone off the bedside table, and went back downstairs as he stabbed out a number he never called but knew by heart.

Winthrop answered. "See-Through Studios."

"Winthrop, it's Dillon McKeon," he said without ceremony. "Let me talk to Harper."

There was silence on the other end as he paced the kitchen, pain knotting and building in his chest.

"I thought she was with you," Winthrop replied finally, concern in his voice. "When did she leave?"

"Winthrop, if they're there and you're preventing me from speaking to her—"

Winthrop interrupted worriedly, "They?"

"Harper and Darian!" he shouted impatiently.

"You...know about him?"

Dillon fought the unreasoning jealousy that Wade had known about the baby. He had to have. There must have been times when Harper had brought Darian to work, times when they'd socialized. And Winthrop had been her friend. That was more than Dillon had been to her.

"I know about him, Wade. Please. Where are they?"

"I'm telling you they're not here, Dillon. When did she leave Dancer's Beach?"

"How the hell would I know?" Dillon returned. "I just got back myself."

"From where?"

Suddenly it was all too much to explain. Dillon simply pushed the off button and slammed the phone onto the countertop. It broke in two in his hand.

He swore, but pulled himself together. Dori would know. All he had to do was wait until Dori got home. She would know when Harper had left and if she'd intended any side trips.

Longing, fury, regret—all raged together in his chest. He hadn't even kissed her goodbye. How dare she take off without telling *him* goodbye! How could a man with the brains and stamina to survive the desperate corners of the world be such a jerk?

Dillon's head turned toward the front of the house at the sudden sound of laughter. He frowned, thinking it was so loud that it sounded like a sitcom laugh track. He tried to pick out the sound of Harper's voice and couldn't.

He strode through the dining room to the living room's front window and saw an incredible sight. It looked like some American tribe of female nomads walking single file down the street, then turning up his driveway.

They all wore shade hats and carried grocery bags. All that was missing were camels. The last one in line pushed a baby carriage. A cellophane bag of oranges rested on the canopy on top.

The laughter changed to the rousing harmony of an old Righteous Brothers tune. The first woman in line threw her head back as she hit a high note, and suddenly the sound and the face revealed by the uplifted brim of the hat were identifiable. But it couldn't be. Harper's aunt Grace?

Grace made the turn in the walk and marching in time with the music, headed for the porch steps. Dillon saw the second in line pause to do a quick tap-step, then raise her face to the sun as she moved on singing. Harper's aunt Edith!

As they turned one by one, he recognized all of them. Aggie. Phyllis on crutches—stopping to wave one of them in the air as they all copied Edith's fancy move—Harper, Cleo with Darian by the hand, Dori.

Harper! Darian!

Dillon yanked the door open and went out onto the porch.

"Dillon! How wonderful that you got home before we had to leave!" Grace took him in her plump embrace. She passed him on to Edith, who passed him on to Aggie, who passed him on to Phyllis, who passed him on to Harper, who sidestepped him and passed him on to Cleo. Darian had a grip on his leg and was shouting "Da-da!" with great authority.

Dillon picked him up and crushed him to him.

He was swept back inside on the cheerful tide of straw-bonneted femininity.

There were more hugs, exclamations, questions. Someone took Darian from him, and handed him Michelle, then Gabrielle. He held them close, remembering with fierce protectiveness the fragile little children he'd repaired in Mexico.

He spoke to them and got wide, toothless smiles.

Then Dori took Michelle, handed her to the nearest aunt, and held Gabrielle herself.

"Welcome home," she said, and under the ruse of a quick hug, whispered as he leaned down to her, "I'll keep Darian and the aunts busy so you can have some time with Harper."

She waved the aunts to follow her. "Family's arriving tonight, so let's get these groceries put away and start on dinner. Jobs for everyone. Come on Dare-devil. Cookies and cocoa!"

Harper moved to join them, but Dillon caught her wrist. She pulled against him, pointing toward the kitchen. Her cheeks were flushed, her eyes wary. "I have to help," she said.

"There are six women in there." He drew her toward him. "I have to talk to you."

She resisted, not looking at all as though she'd missed him. But at least she was here.

"Later," she said.

He pulled a little harder. "Now."

He didn't stop until he had her up against him and could smell her lily-of-the-valley fragrance, see the sparks of silver in her eyes, feel her thigh lean against his as she fought to avoid touching him and succeeded only in falling against him.

"I...we've...had a lot of company while you were gone," she said.

"I can see that."

"No, I mean..."

He didn't want to know what she meant about company. And he didn't want to tell her what he had to tell her just a few yards away from half a dozen interested and probably eavesdropping women.

"Let's go down to the beach," he said.

"No." She shook her head impatiently. "We have a house full of company, dinner to—"

That was as far as she got before he put his shoulder to her waist and lifted her off her feet.

Chapter Fourteen

Harper squared off with him the moment he set her on her feet in the warm sand. "Damn it, Dillon!" she shouted. "This is where I came in! Nothing's changed a bit in all those weeks of trying to make sense of you!"

She was furious at his assumption of control, enormously relieved to see him safe and sound, despondent over the way they'd left each other, and terrified that the resolution she'd made when Allison left might come to nothing after all.

"Yes, it has." He allowed himself a moment to drink in the wonder of her presence when he'd been so sure she'd left him. Then he caught her hand and pulled her with him as he headed for the water's edge. "I had to be without you an entire week, which was hell enough. I had to see sick and broken children, which is always more than I can stand but was particularly hard this time because I know what it's like now to love a child and could really relate to the parents' suffering." He stopped them a small distance from the lacy riffles of water and drew her in front of him. His expression changed from grimly reminiscent to wryly self-deprecating. "And I had to listen to Darrick analyze me and tell me I was running from you, just as you once suggested. That I was thwarting our relationship because I didn't think I deserved to be happy—" he sighed as though the words hurt "—because of Donovan."

She saw conciliation in him, but was afraid to believe it. Could this finally be happening after all this time? "And you're turning over a new leaf by hauling me off like a roll of old carpet?" she asked mildly.

He smiled at that. "That was exuberance. I was so sure you'd left me, but there you and Darian were, marching up the front walk with all the other refugees from *A Chorus Line*."

She frowned at him. "I wouldn't have left Dori to cope alone."

"But you knew I was on my way home. I was cruel to you before I left." He made that admission apologetically. "I was sure you'd taken Darian and gone. Your room and your closet are empty."

"I needed room for my aunts."

"But no one's clothes are in there."

He did look worried about that. Harper allowed herself to smile. "Edith and Grace are in that room. They've lived on the road so long that they live out of their suitcases quite literally. They don't hang things up or put them in drawers so they won't forget them. Their suitcases are stashed under the bed."

He accepted that with a nod. "Then where are *your* things?"

She fidgeted and kicked the toe of her tenny at the sand. "I put them in your room."

He hesitated for several seconds. "To make room for the aunts?" he finally asked.

She looked up at him, sweeping away the distance

she'd been trying to keep from him since she'd walked up the steps and seen him standing on the porch. She hadn't thought then that she could let him know how much she'd missed him; how much she wanted to resolve things between them; how right she thought Allison probably was about her—now that she'd had time to reflect on it.

But he'd admitted that he'd been wrong. She could be no less generous.

"No," she said, letting her love show in her eyes. "To make room for me—with you."

He stared a moment, then folded his arms and asked quietly, "Could you clarify that for me? I know what I want it to mean, but I'd hate to be wrong about it."

"Someone told me while you were away," she said, looping her arm in his and leading him beside her along the beach, "that you couldn't make me secure in your love. That *I* have to believe in it or I'll never feel secure no matter what you do. So I've been thinking about it a lot and finally decided that it isn't fair of me to expect you to live your life in a way that will make up for what I feel I've missed in mine."

He pulled her to a stop, his eyes filled with love and tenderness. "I grew up surrounded by all the things you never had. I should have been more understanding."

She shrugged. "Maybe I should have been less whiny. All I could remember was always being shuttled from aunt to aunt. But when the aunts talk about my time spent with them, they're all thrilled that they got to 'share' me. I'm going to think about it that way from now on. It's all in your perspective. As a photographer, I should have remembered that."

Dillon put a hand to his heart as a bright smile parted

his lips. "Well, listen to us. Do I hear—" he pretended to listen "—wedding bells?"

Harper's heart rose into her throat. "Do you?"

He pulled her to him, her back to his chest, and wrapped his arms around her. He leaned over her until his lips were at her ear, and he pointed to the house. "In that direction. Hear them?"

She leaned back against him and lifted her face for his kiss. "I do," she whispered.

When he finally raised his head, she remembered that she had something momentous—something painful—to tell him.

He looked into her suddenly changed expression and asked warily. "What?"

She sat down on the sand and pulled him down to face her. She held both his hands and said carefully, "Allison came while you were gone."

Dillon felt the blow of that news. After thinking Harper had left him, then discovering she hadn't, but loved him after all, now he was not prepared to sink into the doldrums over other news.

But he had to know. They had to deal with it.

Harper squeezed his hands. "The twins are not Allison's."

It took him a moment to realize why she was sad about that. The twins weren't Allison's so there was no danger of Allison wanting to claim them and him as Harper had feared. So what was the problem?

And then it struck him. That meant the twins weren't his, either. They had to be Duncan's.

Dillon felt dispossessed, bereaved. For a moment the sensation was so enormous that all he could see were Michelle's and Gabrielle's faces snuggled against his arm, or smiling up at him. And he didn't think he could stand it.

He put a hand to his mouth, about to lose his composure.

Harper rose onto her knees, tears streaming down her face, and wrapped him in her arms. "I'm sorry," she wept. "I'm really so sorry. I'd almost rather have lost you to her than have you lose them. Except that Darian would have been devastated if you were gone."

He pulled her down into his lap and they rocked each other. "Please don't talk about losing each other. I knew there was a chance the twins weren't mine, but I had pretty much convinced myself..." He had to stop when his voice began to fail.

He remembered Darrick and Skye's looks of devastation as they'd handed the twins to him when it was time for them to go home. He'd sympathized, but he'd had no idea what the pain was like. Now he did.

"You have Darian," she reminded him, sniffing and sitting back on his knee. "And we'll get to be the twins' aunt and uncle, and we'll give them and David even more cousins to play with."

He buried his face in her throat, absorbing her fragrance, her understanding, her love. "That'd be good," he said. "Very good." He drew a breath and remembered that he had far too much for which to be thankful to be feeling sorry for himself. "Duncan's a great guy. He'll make a wonderful father—if he ever gets home. So I guess they're ours, at least until then."

She kissed him again and smiled into his eyes, her own framed by eyelashes spiked from her tears. "I'm so glad you're home. Allison's the one who told me that I had to find security within myself. I promise never to complain about your going off with the team again, and I can make Darian understand when he's old enough. But, God, I'm so happy to have you back. And maybe we should have the wedding right after the weekend while everyone's here so that if anything happens and you're gone again, I'll be yours and you'll be mine.''

He kissed her soundly, then held her close. ''We've belonged to each other since the day you backed into me. We just weren't smart enough to know it. But we are now. Forever, Harper.''

She held him tightly. ''Forever, Dillon.''

They made the announcement at dinner that night when the senior McKeons, Darrick, Skye and David, and the Fishers joined them and Dori and the aunts for cold cuts and salads in the backyard. Darian had claimed his place in Dillon's lap and was watching the action sleepily.

The cheers were raucous. Peg and Skye and the aunts all cried.

''You have to wear the dress!'' Aunt Grace said.

''But it's only a bodice,'' Skye laughed.

''No.'' Dori handed Gabrielle to Skye as she stood. ''Bertie gave Harper some old white silk and Harper made a skirt for it. I'll go get it.''

Skye came to hug Harper. ''*Can* you wear it?''

''I'm too short for it,'' Harper said regretfully. ''It's for someone taller and longer-waisted.'' She leaned over to kiss Dillon. ''But it worked its magic for me already.''

''All *right!*'' Skye cheered and started the applause again.

The careful viewing of the dress brought up the new discoveries about it and soon the photos and the other items from Fran's envelope were circulating. Aggie, who had made the discovery, pointed out the beadwork on the christening gown that matched the wedding dress.

"So our theory is, there was a skirt," Harper supplied, "but it was removed to make the christening dress for Olivia's baby."

Dillon exchanged a look with Darrick. "And how do we know it was for *Olivia's* baby?" Dillon asked.

"Have we even proven that Barton ever found her?"

Harper and Skye, heads together over the photos, looked up to smile.

"No," Skye admitted. "No proof yet. But we believe. And Gracie has friends in Alaska checking for evidence of Barton or Olivia. It could be a while."

"And the dress has done so much for us." Harper indicated Skye and herself. "Imagine what it must have done for the woman who made it in the first place."

Dillon turned to Darrick with a pained expression. "Can you fight that with logic?"

Darrick shook his head. "Not me."

David climbed into Darrick's lap. "What's logic?" he asked.

"Something your mother's unfamiliar with," Darrick replied, settling the boy in the crook of his arm.

"But she's nice and pretty," David supported Skye staunchly. "And she can fly a plane. So whatever that is, maybe she doesn't need it."

The women cheered, and the men, greatly outnumbered, studied one another in good-humored defeat.

The sound had just quieted when high-pitched screams came from the front of the house. Everyone raced around to the walk that ran between the house and the garage.

Dillon, in the lead, stopped halfway to the street, his

followers bumping into one another like dominoes. Everyone gasped at the sight of a stretch limo pulled up in front of the house. A tall man, with dark hair, dressed completely in white except for a pair of sunglasses, had a suitcase in one hand and held the limo door with the other. He leaned in, and began talking to someone.

The limo had apparently been followed through the neighborhood by women on foot. Thirty or so were gathered around the vehicle, jumping up and down and screaming and giggling excitedly.

The man nodded at whomever he spoke to in the limo. "I'll let you know by August first," he said. "Bye, Steven."

He pushed the door closed and cautioned the young women to move out of the way so the car could accelerate.

The limo proceeded down the block toward the highway, looking weirdly out of place in quiet, unpretentious little Dancer's Beach.

"Thank you, ladies," the man said to the group gathered around him. "I love you, too." A shriek rose from them. "But I'm on vacation for the next few weeks."

They closed in around him and he was forced to wade his way through, smiling and answering questions as he kept moving toward the house.

He was tall in his white T-shirt and slacks, elegantly groomed, and drop-dead gorgeous.

Skye leaned toward Harper and whispered, "Duncan?"

Harper grinned fondly. "That's Duncan, all right."

The McKeons were all together once more, she

thought as Dillon and Darrick went to help extricate him from his admirers. What would follow was bound to be interesting—and hopefully filled with answers.

* * * * *

Look for DADDY BY DESTINY, AR #746, the romantic conclusion to Muriel Jensen's WHO'S THE DADDY? *series, coming to your favorite bookstore October 1998.*

HARLEQUIN®

AMERICAN ◆ ROMANCE®

*Under an assumed name, a woman delivers
twins at Oregon's Valley Memorial
Hospital, only to disappear...leaving
behind the cooing twin girls and a note
listing their dad as D. K. McKeon. Only
trouble is, there are three D. K. McKeons....*

So the question is

Muriel Jensen
brings you a delightfully funny trilogy of
one mystery, two gurgling babies and
three possible daddies!

WHO'S THE
DADDY?

Don't miss:

#737 DADDY BY DEFAULT
(August 1998)

#742 DADDY BY DESIGN
(September 1998)

#746 DADDY BY DESTINY
(October 1998)

HARLEQUIN®

Makes any time special ™

Take 2 bestselling love stories FREE

Plus get a FREE surprise gift!

Special Limited-Time Offer

Mail to Harlequin Reader Service®

3010 Walden Avenue
P.O. Box 1867
Buffalo, N.Y. 14240-1867

YES! Please send me 2 free Harlequin American Romance® novels and my free surprise gift. Then send me 4 brand-new novels every month, which I will receive months before they appear in bookstores. Bill me at the low price of $3.34 each plus 25¢ delivery and applicable sales tax, if any.* That's the complete price, and a saving of over 10% off the cover prices—quite a bargain! I understand that accepting the books and gift places me under no obligation ever to buy any books. I can always return a shipment and cancel at any time. Even if I never buy another book from Harlequin, the 2 free books and the surprise gift are mine to keep forever.

154 HEN CH7E

Name	(PLEASE PRINT)	
Address	Apt. No.	
City	State	Zip

This offer is limited to one order per household and not valid to present Harlequin American Romance® subscribers. *Terms and prices are subject to change without notice. Sales tax applicable in N.Y.

UAMER-98

©1990 Harlequin Enterprises Limited

Intense, dazzling, isolated...

THE AUSTRALIANS

Stories of romance Australian-style, guaranteed to
fulfill that sense of adventure!

This October, look for

Beguiled and Bedazzled
by **Victoria Gordon**

Colleen Ferrar is a woman who always gets what she wants—
that is, until she meets Devon Burns, who lives in the very
secluded Tasmanian bush. He has a proposal of his own, and
the question is: how far will Colleen go to get what she wants?

*The Wonder from Down Under: where spirited women win
the hearts of Australia's most independent men!*

Available October 1998
at your favorite retail outlet.

HARLEQUIN®
Makes any time special ™

THE RANDALL MEN ARE BACK!

Those hard-ridin', good-lovin' cowboys who lassoed your heart—Jake, Chad, Brett and Pete Randall—are about to welcome a long-lost kin to their Wyoming corral—Griffin Randall.

Big brother Jake has married off all of his brothers—and himself. How long can Griffin escape Jake's matchmaking reins?

Find out in
COWBOY COME HOME
by Judy Christenberry

*They give new meaning
to the term "gettin' hitched"!*

Available at your favorite retail outlet.

HARLEQUIN®
Makes any time special ™

Can tossing a coin in the Trevi Fountain really make wishes come true? Three average American women are about to find out when they throw...

3 COINS IN A FOUNTAIN

For Gina, Libby and Jessie, the trip to Rome wasn't what they'd expected. They went seeking romance and ended up finding disaster! What harm could throwing a coin bring?

IF WISHES WERE HUSBANDS...
Debbi Rawlins—September

IF WISHES WERE WEDDINGS...
Karen Toller Whittenburg—October

IF WISHES WERE DADDIES...
Jo Leigh—November

3 COINS IN A FOUNTAIN
If wishes could come true...

HARLEQUIN®
Makes any time special ™

Available at your favorite retail outlet.